FERRY BACK
THE GIFTS

T0159832

FERRY BACK THE GIFTS

KATE STORY

EXILE
e d i t i o n s

singular fiction, poetry, nonfiction, translation, drama, and graphic books

Library and Archives Canada Cataloguing in Publication

Title: Ferry back the gifts / Kate Story.
Names: Story, Kate, author.
Description: Short stories.
Identifiers: Canadiana (print) 2022040562X | Canadiana (ebook) 20220405662 |
ISBN 9781550969573
    (softcover) | ISBN 9781550969580 (EPUB) | ISBN 9781550969597 (Kindle) |
ISBN 9781550969603 (PDF)
Classification: LCC PS8637.T677 F47 2022 | DDC C813/.6—dc23

Copyright © Kate Story, 2022
Cover and pages designed by Michael Callaghan
Typeset in Garamond and Hyper heliX fonts at Moons of Jupiter Studios
Published by Exile Editions Ltd ~ www.ExileEditions.com
144483 Southgate Road 14 – GD, Holstein, Ontario, N0G 2A0
Printed and bound in Canada by Imprimerie Gauvin

We gratefully acknowledge the financial support of the Canada Council for the Arts,
the Government of Canada, and Ontario Creates toward our publishing activities.

Canadian sales representation:
The Canadian Manda Group,
664 Annette Street, Toronto ON M6S 2C8.
www.mandagroup.com 416 516 0911

North American and international
distribution, and U.S. sales:
Independent Publishers Group,
814 North Franklin Street,
Chicago IL 60610 www.ipgbook.com
toll free: 1 800 888 4741

FSC
MIX
Paper
FSC® C100212
www.fsc.org

"Fortune brings in some boats that are not steer'd."

—*Cymbeline*, WILLIAM SHAKESPEARE

Anniversary

Lee woke at dawn, the freeze running through her, full of that 6 a.m. intelligence. Still alive. She knew what she'd been after with that girl the night before: flying above, reaching down, feeling good. Then the pain hit like a fist and she puked it out in the toilet bowl. Sound like a barking dog coming out of her. She slept again on the bathroom floor and woke to more. Hours like this, sun rising cold from the east and hitting the black twisted trees and buildings of the shithole Ontario town, traffic squeezing by – calming – another surge at noon. Lee lay on the bathroom floor wrapped in a dirty blanket and heard it all.

Finally, the floor got to her. A shower, scrubbing down her body: small breasts, incipient beer gut, long lean legs and big feet. Water ran over her, hot, but nothing ran away with the feeling. Lee felt like she could stream out into the naked icy air, run down the street screaming until her tongue and lips and throat turned themselves inside out and her lungs flapped on the outside of her chest like a flayed eagle, spraying blood. Run until the blood was all on the outside and it froze, the only bright thing in that dirty icy January.

A comb through short hair, steam filling the bathroom, pulling on jeans and a white T-shirt, army boots. Motorcycle jacket, the one with a tear down near the bottom, metal zipper coming loose. Sunglasses. Early afternoon now; she walked down the street. No running, lungs inside. Cold, even the creek was frozen solid. The sun burnt shapes into her retina, something twisting down the street in front of her, a pale shape like a bride, a dog. Down to the bar, Lee a bridegroom to the day.

The smell was a wave, grease and booze. Early afternoon piss-poor winter sunlight seeping through the windows; hardly anyone there, she was grateful. Dan pulled a pint for her. It's been a long time since I had a Sunday off, she offered, a sort of excuse although she knew she didn't need to make one, not to him. The pint was in front of her and she drank. Jolt of the first drink of the day like coffee. Gut wrenched and she remembered the blood in the toilet. It was happening more often now – the pain, the blood – another swallow fixed that. Alcohol making her feel alive. She'd always thought she'd be dead before 30, yet here she was, almost a decade past her due date.

The whole bar was busy, a trick of the eye; the owner papered it with reproduction paintings. Chagalls and Van Goghs and giant framed photos of the Stones. She never noticed them anymore but that Chagall behind the bar jumped out at her in the sun today. Blank bride faced out like a doll, and the purple-suited bridegroom carried her in his arms. Flying over the village, animals flying with them. Her blank face like the moon, like Selena. One year ago today but Lee's body was still there on the ground in the white, white snow, trying to hold on to Selena's holy paleness.

Door opened and Dan bounced off to serve the new people. Lee was alone; no, out on the patio for a smoke. The cold hit again, burning; she zipped the jacket all the way up, felt her scalp freeze. Round tables and benches all covered in a thick, soft layer of snow; they looked like giant toadstools, fungi, reaching secret filaments down into the earth, the past, a terrestrial intelligence. They've kept the records of it all. Seven years of nocturnal emissions: whispers, breakups, liaisons, heartbreaks. Piss and puke and spit, beer and booze. Cancers, pregnancies, breath, years of drinking and talking. Lunar wisdom, even frozen you could smell it under the rutted ice. First come-on to Selena over there, a table by the creek.

Springtime then. Everything's thawing, Selena'd said, it's all coming back. Taking her hand and tracing a spiral around her palm. And Lee had thought, *This girl, this is a girl I could change for.* Big green eyes like a cat and long, slender fingers. Her short, blonde hair sticking out in all directions like pale sprouts made Lee want to run her fingers through. Her light, laughing voice.

There were seven creeks in this town, all underneath the grid; seven creeks running with the land, as creeks do. The spring she and Selena got together there was a flash flood and they burst their banks, especially this one, here by the patio where it ran out from the car wash to the north. Running invisible under most of town. It heaved up and turned this patio on its side, took out basements, apartments, windows shattering with the force.

Back inside, trying not to shudder, hands cupped.

3

How'd you make out last night? and Dan wasn't asking about the shift – he took an abnormal interest in her conquests, insecure about himself or something – so Lee answered like it was the shift he was asking about. Busy, she said, and it had been, one of those January nights where it seems the tribe can't take it anymore and drinks to oblivion.

Yeah, but how did *you* make out?

Whole fucking village must be mouthing intelligences. Fuck off, Lee said, draining the last of her pint. Dan poured another, not needing to ask. Lee enjoyed the status of honorary male; boys talked about women around her like she was one of them and she almost was, nearly six feet tall, spare and muscular, brown skin and short, thick hair, going a little grey now. Honourary. She wasn't going to gossip about that poor girl, that failure. Dan smiled, punched her shoulder, saying, Maybe you should pick on someone your own age.

The baby was lucky he was working; Lee could have smacked him. Instead, she paraphrased some Hollywood star: Look, there comes a time in your life when women your own age just seem fucking ancient. She drank some of pint number two. You'll see, little grasshopper, she dismissed him. She wanted to be alone now, now that the beer was taking a bit of a hold. But then that girl came into her head again, last night at the bar. Crying because her boyfriend had dumped her. Lee had flirted across the bar all night, knew the girl from around but never thought of her before, but then that sadness – the magic crept up. Honey, you're beautiful, Lee told her, plastic stuff but she needed it. And Lee was a celebrity with the young ones, the hard-bitten dyke bartender (she used to be a trucker you know!) and all night long they called her name and she delivered what they wanted. What glamour. Sometimes Lee would finish a shift and go home alone and sit in a dark room, nothing, no TV, no radio, no music, no light. Silence. She got so sick of hearing her own name all night long. But the money was good and she'd been at it for a few years now. Seven in fact.

It had been easy. Feeding her drinks, last call and sharing shots. The meaningful eye contact. You need something from the doctor, Lee had said, and they drank to moving on, lady's choice. Then Lee said, Dr. Zeppelin is the cure and it's "Ramble On." Bonham's deceptive tapping, the mellow guitar, Robert Plant's voice soaring over it all and then it broke out. *'Round the world… find my girl… find the queen of all my dreams.* The bar finally cleared out and Lee was almost there. Sent her co-worker home, held the girl's fingers across the bar. Put that song on again, she said, and Lee did, held her close, dancing now but no kiss, not yet. Lee took her home to do that. And she was thinking, *It's so easy to see what they want.*

She flexed her hand, digging nails into her palm. When she was 15, a scarf-clad charlatan in Kensington Market read her palm. Jesus, your lifeline, it's short. Lee had laughed, even back then ready to die. But faint in the sunshine now she saw the woman was wrong: the line drifted on, curving around the base of her thumb, faint as borrowed time, following the memory of Selena's spiral tracery.

A shadow passed through the pale sunlight on her back. She turned, but nothing. The sun lay a little lower now, short winter day. A shudder ran through, she hunched back over her beer. Something dancing over her eyes, a shape, a pale shadow over the bar, obscuring the backlit booze, that holy beer-fridge window. Twisting like a dancer, a dog. Lee remembered an old guy, trucker from when that was her life. He was like something out of a movie of the week, huge gut, one eye gone pale and milky, but somehow, still had his job. She was taking a load of steel across Texas. Her tag had been "Little Dictator," she handled herself well. Break at a truck stop, this one-eyed old-timer talking, going on. And then he told her, *Stop driving when you see the white dog.* Spun out on pills and adrenaline, but she remembered that. Stop. She didn't dictate anything to him that night, old bear, old man.

Lee drank.

At first it had felt good, last night. Another fling to keep her warm. The girl's pretty round face, pale like Selena but Lee didn't go there, not yet. Kisses and heat tightened, one full year poured into her, the girl was the bride and they flew far. Lee anticipated days of fucking; she loved that, how intensely things began, she could get away from the moon for a while. Felt the heat between those legs, she could make the girl pant for more and she did, contorting under her hands, the smell, the taste, her tongue.

And then the shadow came. Lee remembered, drank, downed her pint. The cold shadow, Lee suddenly wanted that girl out of there, out, away, now. Twisted a hand inside her, made her cry out, fucked her thoroughly then threw clothes at her and threw her out. Drunk, half-crying maybe, Lee didn't care to remember. Why, why? Nothing. Just get the fuck out, goodfuckitybye.

Another drink from the Tigger. Sun pretending warmth on Lee's back, liquid slipping down her throat. The bar slowly filled up and Lee was there, the sentinel, holding court. Feeling good now, okay, 5 p.m. on a Sunday and it was the drinkers, the committed ones, drinking the night away to face an intolerable Monday. Lee talked to this one, that one. Dialogue like a thousand small beaks tapping on the outside of her pint glass. Out to smoke and someone's bumming a cigarette.

Still, that table, over there, where it began. Creek silent now, hard blackness of ice. Lee remembered. Moving Selena out of her flood-wrecked place, the sodden rug that she loved and refused to throw away even though the city announced there might be contamination from sewage. They hung that rug from Lee's fire escape for a week and then Selena'd pronounced it sanitized.

Lee couldn't remember what she'd done with that rug afterwards. The smoke-bum was tapping at the windows of her ears. Had she thrown it out in the rage? Into the creek, maybe. Woolen flowers twisting under there now, pink and orange and green as a shipwreck. Can't think like this, can't think of this, it cost her but she pushed the shapes into the background. Talked. Cold, sure, let's go back inside. Ordering a round, shapes receding, good. But then the memory sledges her in the gut: the drive, out in the countryside.

That's what she'd called it, city girl; for Lee it was where she'd grown up, why'd you want to drive anywhere to see it? But they had, leaving the whole village behind, sun on snow like a sea of light. Stopping in some terrible bar in Havelock for beers, night falling. They'd driven back to town, Selena falling into sleep against the passenger window. Selena made Lee want to live. First time that happened. I want to live, live long now, she offered up the body-busting love shining through her and said it out loud to the humming night.

But then the dread crept in – like a nightmare, Lee remembered wanting to say Selena's name but her throat closed, she hadn't been able to speak. And then that white shape, twisting along the road in front, blurring the edges. It had felt like floating, like driving into a flash of light. Lee couldn't remember getting them home; Selena never knew what Lee fought that whole long night-ride. White demon, the dog. They got home and Lee had carried Selena up over the stairs and into the apartment, loved her until she came hard, that white holy body of hers. Fingers digging, cold yearning, desperate searching for the darkest shade of heat inside of her. You make love like it's religion, she'd said to Lee lying back on snowbound sheets, sweat-crowned.

It had been another drive, weeks later for no reason, that had been the one. No dread felt then, nothing. Snow on the ground. Come on, let's go to that bar again Selena begged. Highway 7, ice. Lee remembered the car fishtailing, no problem she could handle that. But the car started spinning on the highway, a nervous giggle from Selena sharpening to a scream. Another car, there's another car. Headlights swerving, *I want to live,* Lee thought, the split second of unbelief, then the smash. Selena hadn't been wearing her seat belt and she flew through the air, a glimmer of blue… Lee imagined this over and over but could only remember the screaming smash of glass and metal. She got out of the car – that, she didn't remember, would never be able to tell how she got there – held that white, broken body under the moon, in the snow, a farmer's field. Perfect, like Chagall.

Kid driving the other car was killed. His girl broke her head and lost a leg. Girl's family tried to bring a court case first against Lee, then the boy's family when it became obvious that he'd been DUI. Pointless exercises in pain. Lee saw the girl around sometimes. They didn't speak. Maimed survivors.

Lee had never expected to survive her life. But she had, she was alive, alone, living on years stolen from Selena. The belief had been growing in her and now she knew it. A life she had and never wanted because Selena had given her everything, because Selena was gone.

Lee walked out of the bar, strode down the length of the place like she was on fire. Faces streamed by like blue flame, eyes tiny sparks, mouths moving but no sound got in over the roaring. Selena, a whole year, leave me will you? Burning couldn't reach the cold thing inside. The shapes wouldn't leave her, latched on. Her hope, repentance, her white dog.

Animate

Laurie makes the nine-hour drive from the city in seven. St. John's to Gros Morne: *great sombre*, mountain standing alone.

The land slips by. Standing stones of the Avalon barrens and rolling terrain of the east flatten out; Deer Lake; farms, fields of hardy wheat, unthinkable even 15 years ago. Finally, the land pushes up into dark peaks, a cast-off, far-flung northeastern arm of the Appalachian range.

They are lucky to live here. In some ways, things in Newfoundland have become – Laurie admits it – easier.

The road winks in and out of shadows, and Laurie watches Daniel sideways. It seems to her that he becomes magnetized. His thick, shiny hair, combed back from forehead to nape, pulls into lines like iron filings dragged across paper, and his lazy eye pulls further to the side.

The immense boreal forest – stretching from Alaska to Siberia, to Japan even –you can feel it watching. It's slowly dying, the forest, in many places, but not on this island. The forest watches. The car slides through the old, worn mountains, beneath hard green eyes.

Daniel sleeps. Signs for the national park begin to appear. Laurie turns on the radio. There's a news story about an inexplicable outbreak of pulmonary edema among the millions of Bangladeshi people resettled in India since their country succumbed. "They're drowning in fluid inside their own bodies," a doctor explains. She says in her lilting English that they can't explain how or why the condition has spread through the refugees, but a geopathologist is interviewed. He posits a psycho-geographic effect, an intangible link between people's bodies and the risen ocean's submergence of their land.

Daniel wakes. He doesn't speak, and as for Laurie, she gave up trying to make conversation as far back as Grand Falls. Daniel is a wreck of a human being, so word goes, and she is newly divorced; they should have everything to say to each other. Silence seeps into the car from the land around them, like water through the timbers of a raft.

They enter the park through a construction zone; they're re-routing the road due to persistent flooding. Replacing asphalt with solar panels; *That's good*, she thinks. *We're finally catching up.* The guy holding the Slow sign jerks his head as Laurie drives past him, and she nods in return.

Daniel speaks. Laurie jumps.

"That sideways thing," he says, "that oblique sort of head-jerk."

He's talking about the construction worker. "It's a bay guy thing," Laurie says.

"What does it mean? Hello?"

"Hello, and a bit of a flirt." She glances over at him. He could be handsome, if he wasn't so knotted around himself. "But to you, because you're a man and we're obviously from St. John's, a bit of a challenge."

11

"I'm not from St. John's."

Daniel's the veterinarian from the mainland. He grew up somewhere in Ontario – it's vague, it's just "the mainland" after all – then practiced in Vancouver. Then the San Andreas finally heaved. He was one of the few survivors of that terrible event. While everyone knew it was due to go, there's a school of thought linking the planet's increased seismic activity to the melting glaciers. Earth's crust bounces back in "isostatic rebound" as the ice thins, seeps, falls, lightens. That makes Daniel another climate refugee.

He aroused a lot of interest in her single friends: new man, *with* a job; and clean, nice manners.

Then his personal faultline cracked. He's been in hiding since.

He needs to learn how to be human again.

One of her friends from work, Karen, suggested Laurie take Daniel on this trip. "We dated, you know, he was nice," she said a touch wistfully. Karen, with her perpetually broken heart; she picks the wrong men, youngsters and drunks and disasters.

She should know better. We're social workers, Laurie thinks, and then remembers that the snug cocoon of her own marriage has split. It opens in her gut, a pit, a piece of her that Jesse took and the hole he left is festering, getting bigger. Laurie closes it over. She's getting better at that. She pictures a pile of stones filling up the hollow putrescence. Stones, one then another, like rocks worn smooth on a beach. They sit heavy in her body. She prefers insensate weight to the hole.

As darkness falls, they pull into a site just in view of Kildevil Mountain. It rises like a shoulder on the other side of a bay, trees patchy, rock shrugging through torn fabric. The rain that's been spitting on them all the way across the island suddenly clears. They set up a tarp over the picnic table as a cooking shelter, tying a ridgeline rope to the convenient overhanging branches of a spruce tree. Then they set up her two-man tent. The sites have been crafted to look natural, but the National Parks gravel lying under the grass makes it hard to sink the tent pegs. Laurie hurts her hand. Daniel is awkward, alternately pulling with too much strength or drifting off. She has to call him back to task three, maybe four times; he keeps staring up at the sky, or at the bay, or at the mountain, still visible as the sun slips under.

The rain comes back as light dies from the sky and so they huddle under the tarp, sitting on the picnic table. She pulls up her hood and hugs her knees. They had stopped at Pizza Hut in Deer Lake, so they're not hungry. It hardly seems worthwhile to light a fire. And she didn't bring any booze, of course, not with Daniel's history.

A mistake — it was a mistake to come.

Vague shouts and singing come wafting from someplace down below. Or across the bay, maybe — hard to tell.

"You hear that?" Daniel says, head cocked. His yellow raincoat is torn, she sees, at the armpit.

"Probably the Christian camp at Kildevil." More and more of them of late; they come here from all over the world to sing down the end of days.

"Did they name the mountain?"

"No, the name's older... I don't know where it came from."

She's rubbing her hand, not even knowing she's doing it, and Daniel takes it between his palms, massaging it.

She freezes.

He drops her hand.

"I'm going for a walk." His figure disappears into the drizzle, the twilight, and she listens to the crunching of his feet on gravel until that disappears into the rush of wind across the bay, through the spruces over her head.

She sits for what seems like a long time. More singing from the Christian camp wafts on the breeze.

She wonders when Daniel will come back. She needs to look after him; it helps her build her stone walls. She's honest enough to admit it; well, and she is hoping to bring him out of his exile too. Waste of a good human, that. The accident wasn't his fault. He was addicted, you have to allow for that sort of thing although Jesse would say that even an addict holds responsibility for—

Rocks slide in her chest, and for a moment it's hard to breathe. She builds herself up again, here, now, woman on a picnic table under a tarp in the rain. When it feels safe again she slips off the picnic table and crouches to pee. Rain rattles on her hood. She heads for the tent; the hell with trying to brush her teeth or anything. She wriggles from her clothes and changes her socks to dry ones, zips into her sleeping bag. Empty one next to her, old one of Jesse's, *shut up*.

Daniel will come back. He's not that deranged.

Stories she's heard from Karen: he hid in his house for months after it happened, drinking and pissing in corners, on the furniture. Behaviour that would have led him, were he an animal under his care, to put himself down.

The wind rises and the trees around the site creak. Laurie lies under the rattling synthetic tent in the rain.

A dream of a creature in a house, howling in the basement. The basement is an empty theatre: rows of old, red velvet seats, a theatre set of painted ocean waves on the back wall. The creature hides among them. The theatre's leaking, water is coming in from all sides and she doesn't know what to do. She goes upstairs, and Karen comes over for tea. They talk over the howling. Trees push up through the floor, hard, dark-green points. The dream devolves into formless emotion that works her jaw, even in sleep.

No telling how much later it is when the tent unzips and something wet and breathing hard rolls inside.

"I hope that's Daniel," she says.

A grunt. Daniel lies down on top of the sleeping bag, muddy boots and wet coat and all. Then he says, "I'm sorry."

Within moments he is snoring. Annoyance; Jesse's sleeping bag will be ruined, all that wet and dirt.

She has to pour rocks into her chest again. She lies there, weighted and suddenly cold, wondering why she thought she could save this wreck of a man snoring and breaking next to her all night long.

She wakes and the light is orange inside the tent, the rain has stopped scratching and rattling. She's alone. Mud streaks on Jesse's sleeping bag, though, she didn't dream that. And she smells woodsmoke. Laurie rolls out of the tent, struggling into boots she left under the fly. It's overcast but not raining. Daniel has gotten a fire going.

"Good morning."

"Hey." Bacon too, he's gotten stuff out of the car and is making breakfast.

No, just bacon. The whole package of it in the pan.

A flash of camping here with Jesse two years ago, and the terrific eggs he used to make, even over a fire.

This enters her. The force of the anger that follows catches inside, a physical pain.

She mutes the feeling, stone by stone, walking toward Daniel across soggy grass. A thought – that this trip feels like some sort of penance for not having been able to keep Jesse – slithers out from some gap in the rocks.

"You want to go for a hike today?"

Daniel nods, pokes at the bacon with a fork. Jerks his head in a passable imitation of the bay-boy nod. "That way." She catches his eye and they both almost smile.

After bacon and instant coffee, Laurie hauls out the park map from her glove compartment. "The Tablelands. You want to go there?"

"Tablelands?" His brown eyes are startled, vague. She wonders now if he managed to bring some kind of drug with him. Some of the horse tranquilizer they found in his veins the night he killed that boy in his car.

"They're in that direction," she points. "Where you said you wanted to go. I've never been on that trail before, but I hear it's nice." She's babbling.

"Nice." He stares through the trees as if he can see the Tablelands from here.

Laurie cleans the pan and then comes back; he's still staring. She puts together a day pack with water, food. She gets in the car. "You coming?"

"Where are you going?"

"To the Tablelands, Daniel. God. Get in the car."

"I thought we were walking," but he uproots himself and clambers into the passenger seat.

"We are. But it's a drive away; the trail starts in Trout River." She looks at him, still in his torn, yellow raincoat. "It's a, maybe, seven-kilometre hiking trail in, and then you come out again; it doesn't loop." She rattles the map. "You up for that?"

He nods, staring out the windshield.

Trout River is gone now. Too much tidal flooding, too many storms. Many communities have been abandoned in what the government calls "a managed retreat." The example of Florida haunts them; the U.S. waited too long before admitting the rising seas weren't going back down.

She doesn't miss it, Trout River; it was always a bit of a hole. Houses, half-built and peeling; the broken windows.

It's a relief to see the Parks Canada sign, all very civilized, in the parking lot outside the old town. They head into the woods, following the markers. Daniel doesn't offer to carry the day pack. Well, what did she expect, a knight?

After a bit the sun comes out from behind clouds and it's unexpectedly hot under the trees, humid and stifling. She stops to drink water, ties her coat around her waist and stuffs her sweater into the day pack. The path meanders up and down: tree roots, slippery rocks, small waterfalls that tumble across the trail. She remembers climbing Gros Morne with Jesse five years ago, and how they almost killed themselves doing the Snug Harbour trail. *Park staff chronically underestimate the difficulty levels of these trails,* Jesse used to say. She remembers that she hasn't reminded Daniel that they need to watch for ticks – that's new – hadn't had any ticks here, not before, the winters used to be too hard… Why can't she stop thinking of how things were before? But the remembering is softer than it has been; the going's hard enough that it hardly hurts to remember, it's a jumble of footsteps, past and now, past and now. Seven kilometres, but the elevation is making it a bit of a challenge, the long, slow climb up to the Tablelands.

"Daniel, do you mind slowing down?" She has to call out, he's gotten so far ahead. He turns.

"Sorry," he calls. He bounds back toward her, almost running. "Sorry."

"It's okay. You want some water?"

He takes the platypus water skin and drinks deeply. He looks along the trail. "There's something…" and he trails off.

"What?"

He lifts his head. "Over that way." He shifts. "Do you feel it?"

"The rock?"

"The watching."

That feeling of being watched, yes. She nods warily. "The forest or…"

"In Ojibwe," he says, "in the language, things are animate or inanimate. Not masculine or feminine, just… wood is animate. And stones." He paused. "No, that's not quite right. To the Anishinaabeg, everything's alive. Animate and inanimate – that's a dichotomy. A very un-Anishinaabe concept."

It's the longest utterance from him this whole trip. She wants to ask if he has any Ojibwe blood in him, but you don't do that. "Animate," she says, looking down, rolling a pale, smooth stone under her foot. She wonders if the First Peoples here think like this too. "What's inanimate?"

"People," he says.

She hopes he is kidding.

His eyes focus on the day pack she's carrying. "Let me take that. Sorry."

They continue. Trout River Pond opens out to their right, too huge for its name, like a fjord. Pure, pure water in there. The trail begins to climb more steeply. Laurie sees caribou scat, and bear. Through a break in the trees she spots two eagles wheeling above the water. Ravens, hidden in the trees, cackle and roll marbles in their throats at the two damaged humans toiling below. If she were hiking with anyone else she'd point all this out, it'd become part of the story of their hike. But with Daniel there is no making a story; his desolation pulls words apart.

They are coming out of the woods, now. Trees die, then bushes, even grass. A vast hump of land soars above them, painfully bright against the blue of empty sky.

Orange rock, weeping rust. No birds here, no animals. The silence is terrible.

Daniel has stopped walking; he stares up at it.

"It's really old," says Laurie, catching her breath. "Some of the oldest rock in the world." She's just saying this to fill the silence.

"Why is it… why does it look like that?"

"It's poisonous."

He looks at her now. That thing she'd noticed on the trip across the island, it's happening again: his eye pulls to the side, his hair strains back over his head in lines, neat as if he'd just combed it, iron filings on paper. How dark his eyes are.

"The rock's from too far below, or something. It doesn't have any nutrients. It's full of heavy metals, or toxic, or something."

"Toxic."

"I'm not a geologist or anything but that's what I remember Jesse telling me." She's said his name.

"Your husband." This slowly, coming from inside him, a memory of meeting at a dinner party maybe, that one at Karen's.

She wants to say *ex* but her tongue is thick.

There's a look on Daniel's face she can't read.

Maybe this is what it's always like for him. Maybe everything is thick, slow, walled up. She imagines kissing him.

He has turned and continued walking. He's got a prowl that is somehow sexual. Attractive. She lets him get quite far ahead before she follows.

The trail climbs up over the Tablelands. It reminds her of Iceland, some of the volcanoes she climbed on that trip with… yeah, with her *ex-husband, Jesse*. She wonders if she'll travel alone now. She wonders if she'll have the guts. No, she can't think ahead, the thoughts will fester in that ripped-open place in her chest. One step, one step, one step. Walking on stones. Daniel far ahead again, she lets him go.

The trail climbs, levels out. They're on top of the Tablelands and she sees the reason for the name. It is flat, level as if a god sheared the top off. The water far below is blue, and on the other side, startling, a hill mounds up as high as the Tablelands. It's a normal hill, covered in green: tuckamores and spruce. Waterfalls tumble down it, far, far. Like Earth next to Mars, the fjord a starry space between.

Daniel's lost to view. She walks. There's something about following a trail: you will go, keep going, because there's a destination. She wonders what the end will be. Maybe there will be something: a look-out, a view. She wishes she had the pack with her still; she's thirsty.

Finally, she sees a blot of yellow up ahead. He's sitting on a rock. Waiting for her? No, it's just that the trail has ended, petering out in the wilderness.

There's a sort of vista, no grander than anything else they've seen: green land and water where the Tableland drops off into air, the red rust of barren rock all around them. Daniel sits staring at the green across the void.

She makes her way to him and sits down, taking water from the pack he's tipped off his shoulders. She drinks, watching as he picks up a red, poisonous rock, hefts it in his hand. He throws the rock; it bounces, tumbles down the slope. "I hate it here." He picks up another rock and tosses it high in the air. It falls out of sight in a pit.

"The Tablelands?" Well, what the hell, she's done her best to please the creature.

"No." He looks her way. "This island. This whole god-damn island."

"Why?"

"It's too cold in the winter. The wind. Goddamn cold."

"Yes." She feels inexplicable laughter bubbling up. "Yes, it is cold in the goddamn winter."

He throws another rock and when this one lands it splits, showing its deep green inside. Daniel stares. "Look!"

"They're all like that. Green inside." Green, like jade, like a secret.

The silence, she feels… It passes, he shifts away again.

She bows her head, rifling through the pack to find the food she brought. She fills her mouth with chocolate. If Laurie were on death row, this would be her last requested meal: fair trade organic, dark.

On the way back, when the trail meanders down to the vast, pure pond's edge, she steps off the trail, onto the rocky shore. She unlaces and kicks off her boots, intending to go wading. Instead, she finds herself walking out and out, feet hurting as stones slip beneath her, sliding like the stones in her chest. The water wicks up her clothes, to her waist, to her chest where the rocks are. The cold insolence creeps into her body.

"You going in?" Daniel's standing on the trail, a poisonous red rock in his hand.

"If you are," she says.

"I'm already in." A smile pulls at his mouth. He cocks his arm, throwing the stone far out into the water, almost boyish. They both watch it disappear, slipping below the surface. "I'm already in."

The ripples from his stone spread, fading. But there's a resurgence, ripples becoming small waves. Laurie feels her hair standing up as if electrified, pulling, back toward the

Tablelands. The ground shifts beneath her feet. She laughs, spreads her arms to keep her balance. Daniel looks back the way they've come. Rocks are sliding down the slopes. A tree begins to walk.

Still laughing, Laurie says, "Daniel, I think it's an earth-quake!"

Isostatic rebound.

She feels her hair coiling like a Medusa's, and as for Daniel, his head is a Sputnik, a straining halo. Daniel too begins to laugh. He does a half-spin and falls spread-eagle into the water.

Laurie doesn't wait to see him come up. She crouches down, lungs shuddering, gulping air. Her clothes are heavy. She lets the water close over her head. Cold. She crouches like an animal on the bottom of the ancient lake, ground shaking, water surging. She feels her weight.

The silence of the sky above and the water below meet inside the shifting earth.

FLAME RETARDED

Flame Retarded, Quality Costumes, Colourful Masks with Wide-Vision Eye-Holes, Brite for Nite!!! I squished my nose against the grimy glass. I wanted it, the ballerina outfit with the white tutu. In my family we got costumes Mom made, or one of a series of ancient Devil costumes passed down from our vast array of older cousins, all of whom apparently wished to go out on Hallowe'en dressed as Satan. But this year, it was ballerina or bust.

I was going out that Hallowe'en night with Lois "Where's-the Loot-Bag" Collins. She was so named because at my fifth birthday party, as soon as she walked through the door, she shrieked in her nasal voice, "Where's the loot bags? *Where's the loot bags?*" She didn't stop until my mother said, "Here's your damn loot bag, Lois-Where's-the-Loot-Bag Collins, for the love of Christ!" The name stuck. Lois was a skinny, little kid with a head of stiff, red hair. I've always had a thing for redheads. Lois-Where's-the Loot-Bag Collins was my first crush, Grade One and Grade Two and Grade Three. It probably would have continued if she hadn't failed Grade Three, staying behind while I moved on to other grades and redheads.

Lois was going out this year as a princess. She'd described her costume to me: "It's all white and long like a bride and there's a cloak and a diamond crown!" *White and long like a bride* – I couldn't walk next to her as a tattered, grubby devil. I was afraid to ask my mother, yet something about Lois's lust for loot must have rubbed off on me for I took my courage in hand and I nagged. I nagged until my mother said "Stop nagging!" and then I whined, and I whined until even I was sick of it, and finally (in a towering rage that did nothing to dampen my utter triumphant joy at getting my sticky hands on that cheap white netting) my mother stormed into the store and bought me "that damn ballerina outfit." Lois's hair was bright like copper and it stuck out in all directions. She'd look beautiful in a diamond crown. We would look wonderful, the princess and the dancer, together.

Yes, I've always had a thing for redheads. My second redhead was Beverly: Beverly of ballet class, Beverly of the long red hair. Thick, so thick that her braid was three inches across, and long, so long it went all the way down to her waist. Beverly was a beautiful dancer but cursed with short legs and big tits; even at the age of 12 it was obvious she wasn't going to have a career in ballet. Even so, she always wore her hair pulled back tight into a bun as if she was about to spring into a tutu and practice *Swan Lake*. Beverly was suicidal and used to run away from home. She'd call me from phone booths: "I'm going to kill myself. I really mean it this time. I don't know where I am. My mother doesn't know I've left the house. I'm going to throw myself in front of a car," and then she'd hang up. I'd sit by the phone in an agony, waiting for her next call. "I'm going to do it now. As soon as a truck goes by." I'd walk for hours in the Newfoundland winter night, looking for her; once she'd walked halfway to Cape Spear before I got to her and coaxed her all the way down Blackhead Road to my house. Our mothers called what we did "Sleepovers." I'd chase her all over town, pluck her from the brink of death, and then we'd go to her house or mine and drink hot chocolate. We'd give each other massages and she'd take her hair out of its bun, and then we'd lie next to each other. I'd be stretched out there on the mattress next to her listening to her breath, and burning up inside.

But before that, before out-growing Hallowe'en and taking real ballet classes and flirting with real anorexia and pointe shoes, there was Lois and the Brite for Nite costume. I walked to the bridge that separated her road from mine, clutching an empty bag for candy, heart pounding. She was already there waiting for me, a white blob in the twilight. I have to say that her costume was, as far as princesses went, a disappointment. It was pretty much the same as mine, except her skirt was longer and she had a cheap tiara on her head, almost lost in her hair. Of course I had my magic wand and, in a burst of genius, a little bag of sparkles that I could throw into the air. "Hi," she said when she saw me. I took a deep breath and wished hard and looked at her again, and because I wanted it enough, she *was* a princess and I was a ballerina and we were beautiful, despite our woolen socks.

We hit every house along the Waterford River between her place and our school. It was a long stretch, maybe a mile, with a cold wind, but we were determined (she wasn't Where's-the-Loot-Bag for nothing). We got pretty close to the school, and then Lois said in her nasal voice, "Hey, I wonder if the perv is around?" and I said, "Naw, b'y," and she said in sepulchral tones (with nasal overlay), "How do you know? I bet he loves Hallowe'en. I bet it's his favourite night!" and I said, "Yeah, he dresses up as the Perv!" and this wasn't very funny, but we laughed, staggering along in each other's arms. And we were indeed close to the school, and there was indeed a perv, and I can't speak as to what his favourite night may have been, but a night when children roam unattended surely couldn't be too far down his list. He was an old man, in his 40s, ancient. He used to hang around in the small clump of trees we called "The Woods" at the top of the hill above our elementary school, and flash little girls. We'd shriek and run away.

It was dark and I spun along the sidewalk ahead of Lois, waving my wand in the air. I was trying to do pirouettes, only I didn't know what pirouettes were yet; this was before Beverly and the ballet classes. And I was trying to be enchanting, and I remember a strange feeling in my six-year-old body, because I was trying to *appear* enchanting. You couldn't be enchanting in a devil costume with a fraying forked tail. But this year I was a ballerina. And I remember feeling a bit sick and strange and at the same time very excited. "I'm dancing, I'm dancing! I'm a beautiful dancer!" I hummed to myself under my breath. "I'm a beautiful dancer!" And I waved my wand and spun my plastic bag full of candy and I hopped up and down. And I sang a little song, and spun some more, and then I looked behind me and the sidewalk was empty; that is to say, there was no one on it except me.

Years later I would be walking along that same stretch of sidewalk alone, only this time it would be a New Year's Eve night, that Hallowe'en of young adulthood. And I'd be dressed in sparkles then too, gold pants, with shine on my décolletage and a good pair of shoes. And I'd be coming home from the house of a red-haired star, well, star in the local sense of the word, a star and a redhead; could I ask for more? I was a good girl, good enough to leave when his girl-friend phoned and I was always so good about it, even when he wouldn't fuck me so he could save himself for her. I'd laughed and spun around, right out the door for him; I could fake a pirouette by then. He had red hair and I burned for him, flame retarded.

And I stood there on that same sidewalk when I was six and the sidewalk was empty of Lois and of anyone, and I said, tentatively, "Lois?" And then she screamed. I knew it was her, even though I couldn't see her – the scream came off the side of the road, in some trees. And I said, "Get off it, that's not funny!" and I started backing away from the scream, and then she screamed again and I turned and ran away up the road, then spun and ran toward her, then away, then toward, back and forth like a little, scared mouse. And then I heard rustling in the bushes and a grunting noise and a sob, sort of choked off. And I'll never know why but I charged into the bushes where the noises were coming from and saw him there in his awful dark coat, and Lois was under him only I couldn't see her face, just a bit of white-ness that was her costume, and he was jerking at her in this awful way. And I shrieked and I hit his back with my little, plastic magic wand. And then I spun around and I hit him again, not exactly pirouetting, because I hadn't learned that yet.

"Get it *right*," the ballet teacher would say to me. "Turn! Turn!" Beverly had so much hair that she had to use those giant metal hairpins to fasten it up in a massive, sleek, ruby bun, and in the recital we spun around and around, only I could never quite do it, and the pins started coming loose from Beverly's hair, and they shot around the stage *ping! ping!* like tiny missiles, like bullets, and the rest of us tried to keep dancing, but they were shooting out at a furious rate now, pinging and zinging and people in the audience started ducking, then a woman cried out, and there was a great roar and confusion and people were flinging themselves into the aisles. One dancer screamed as a metal pin pierced her white-feathered breast. Blood blossomed around it and she fainted. We other dancers fled, the audience trampled each other in their panic, and at the center of it all was Beverly, spinning, spinning and the light on her grew whiter and brighter, metal shot out from her hair like steel hornets and she glowed, seemed to rise from the ground in her spinning, a vortex of light and weaponry until her hair finally came loose and spread around her shining red like ruby jewels, like fire, like blood and joy, and she spun up and through the roof of the Arts and Culture Centre, blood angel ascending to heaven.

Years later it all got written about in the newspaper – not Beverly the Blood Angel, that was too strange and too wonderful and those who had been there could never agree on what had happened. What got written about was the perv and all us girls at the school, and there was an interview with Lois's mother wherein she wept and said she grew up back when you really didn't talk about those things; I mean, we just didn't *know* about those things. And after failing Grade Three Lois and I sort of lost track of each other, but the newspaper article – my mother showed it to me – went on and on with the usual story: how she got sullen and difficult and stopped doing well in school. And then she started doing drugs and had an abusive boyfriend and left home and her mother didn't know where she was. And my mother was very grave as she showed me this, and she wanted to talk about it. She said she hadn't realized… had it… had I… was that why…?

"Why *what?*" I said.

And that was the end of that.

Years later as I walked along that sidewalk, bleeding, it was still dark and I couldn't remember exactly where it had happened. Was it here? Or here? Or those bushes in there? It being New Year's Eve in St. John's there were three different cabbies who slowed down and offered me a ride home. "No thanks, I don't mind the walk." *I need to walk off my sweet-temper. It's making me sick.* "If it's a question of money, me luv, don't worry; hop in, I've made enough tonight." "Aw, thanks, but I'm nearly home." I'd never be able to find the place again, so much had grown over it, it'd been years and I still hadn't learned to pirouette, had, in fact, given up trying.

But once, one Hallowe'en night, I'd danced around Lois and the man. I'd spun with my wand and my tutu. I'd thrown sparkles. I didn't know then that those would be the best spins I'd ever do. The perv ran away. Lois sat up. We walked home together. We didn't talk. We were covered in sparkles. We shone.

WHERE THE SEAS ROLL UP THEIR THUNDER

Am I close enough? The microphone is built right in, is it?

Clever little technologies they have these days.

So, you're here about the Bell Island Boom. What made you want to talk to me in particular?

Smart? Well, odd, or eccentric, that's more what I'm used to hearing about myself. Or worse. But smart. I like that. It's true, I always have my nose in a book. Always was like that. I used to love reading those old science fiction paperbacks. They had a soft feeling, the pages, and a musty smell. Must be the cheap paper. Do you read much? I used to go into St. John's to get the books, because you couldn't get them here, not on Bell Island. Not a bookshop in the place, me love. My brothers called me "Bookworm," because I always had my nose in a book. Original jokesters, my brothers.

I was very fond now of books about Mars. Martians. There are so many of them. The *Barsoom* series. *Red Planet*. Have you noticed how we humans seem to recycle ideas? Like this idea, that somewhere and sometime on Mars there was this vast civilization. There's a sadness to our imagining. A sadness to it all, yes, nostalgia. Nobody does nostalgia like Newfoundland. *Take me back to my western boat. Let me fish off Cape St. Mary's…*

What's that face, me duckie? Don't you like my singing? *Take me back to that snug green cove, where the seas roll up their thunder…*

All right, all right, I'll get around to the Boom. We'll start at the beginning. That's what your high-school teacher wants, right, for the project? Names and dates and all that.

My name is Susan Fitzgerald. I was born in 1935, and… Yes, 1935. I am 82 years old.

You look disappointed. Aren't I old enough? What's that? Someone told you I was a hundred?

No, me son. I'm not a hundred. My. I haven't laughed like that in a long time.

You're here now, aren't you? Have another cookie.

1978, now, that's when it was. I'm old enough to remember that, certainly. How old do you think I was when it happened? Or aren't they teaching you math anymore?

Very good, I was 43. Still fairly ancient.

Well, it was very unexpected. For most people that is.

Yes, it was a Sunday morning. A lot of people were in church.

No. I was down on the beach. The Grebe's Nest. The Grebe… A grebe is a bird, a migratory bird. It summers here, raises its young, then travels vast distances, almost unimaginable, all the way over to Europe… migratory. Migratory… Your mother's from here, isn't she? From this town, from Wabana? Before her people moved to Portugal

Cove, after the mine closed, yes, I knew your mother. I'd have thought she'd have taken you down to the Grebe's Nest at least once.

I used to lie in the grass on the cliff tops overlooking the Grebe's Nest, grass and wild strawberries, roses and vetch, and stare up into the sky, and wait for ancient aliens to come get me.

I knew if I wished hard enough, they would come. Because I was special, chosen. Oh, yes, we seem to recycle that idea too, don't we? These ideas that come up over and over again, like being chosen… Does the mouse dream the dream of the cat?

The Grebe's Nest is over that way. No, we can't see it from here. It's a bit of a walk, up past the Number Two mine, along Carter Avenue and past Mr. Crane's place, then it sort of peters out into a path. It's a lovely little sandy beach, sheltered, and many of the rocks have fossils…

Didn't I say? Just that it's shaped like a nest. That's all. It's a little crescent moon of a place. Magical. A lot of people say that about it, not just me.

In the old days, miners living nearby used to supplement their income with some fishing, and they'd bring their catches into the Grebe's Nest. It was an easy place to drag a dory onto shore. But the cliffs are high there. I'd say over a hundred feet. They attached a cable and they'd send their catch up in tubs, to the top, pulled by a horse. Then row around and home again. You could get to a nearby beach just by walking, but that beach is rough and rocky, unsheltered – no good for boats. So, in the sixties, after all the Bell Island mines closed, the miners had a lot of time on their hands and a lot of mining experience. Not to mention a lot of explosives. So, they blasted through the point of land that separated the Grebe's Nest from the path. Maybe a hundred and fifty feet, the tunnel. No, I wouldn't exactly call it safe. Maybe that's why your mother hasn't taken you there. We can go after we finish talking, if you like.

Which we'll never finish doing if I don't stick to the point. Sunday morning, right. April 2, 1978. There was snow on the ground. I was down in the Grebe's Nest, and everybody else was in church.

Everything got quiet. The wind dropped. The sea even seemed to pause. And then, the air filled with this ringing. Like a tone, like a bell.

And then I saw something in the sky. It could have been a meteor, yes.

The Boom rocked the island, like an electrical shock. It shook the island, me duckie. They heard it 60 miles away. That's a hundred kilometres.

Electrical appliances burst apart. Blue flame shot out of electrical outlets. Animals fell over dead. Buildings were rent asunder. The explosion was loud, the loudest sound anyone had ever heard, louder even than the German torpedoes back in 1942... I'll tell you about those later, me love. No, I don't believe they ever found an epicentre to the explosion. All that was left – other than some dead chickens with blood seeping out their eyes and beaks, and some burnt-out appliances and startled people – was some holes in the snow, and two small hollows in the ground.

Mr. and Mrs. Bickford's wee grandson saw a great globe of light, hovering above the ground. But nobody else saw anything like that.

What's that? A beam of light?

Yes, there was a woman over across Conception Bay swore that she saw a beam of light shooting up from the ground. But I believe they didn't hold much by her testimony.

Certainly, there were lots of stories.

You've heard about Mr. Warren and Mr. Freyman, have you? People got very excited when they came. Yes, that's right, from the Los Alamos Scientific Laboratory in New Mexico. They started asking around.

Because of their suits perhaps, people thought they worked for the U.S. Government.

It turned out they were tracking... lightning super bolts, that's right, you've done your homework. They told everyone that they were satisfied the boom had been a lightning super bolt, and they went back to New Mexico.

Yes, it struck near Lance Cove. Pretty much the opposite end of the island from the Grebe's Nest.

No, I didn't speak to them. I was in hospital in St. John's. See this hand? Yes, that's a burn. I still can't close it properly.

How did it happen?

A burn, what do you think?

No, I never thought anything like that.

Who's that? Nikola Tesla, who's that?

I see. A doomsday device. But who'd develop a doomsday device?

Well yes, I suppose the U.S. or the Soviets might have had an interest back then… But who'd shoot a doomsday device at Bickford's old farm?

Ah, the iron ore. Yes, me son, Bell Island's riddled with it. Great blood-coloured layers of it all through the rock. It's heavy. Here, hold this in your hand. Heavy, isn't it? That's the iron makes it so. But there's a flaw in your theory, I think, me duckie. Iron ore isn't a magnet. Just try and draw something with that rock you're holding. It's *magnetic,* certainly, and it can be magnetized, but it's not in and of itself a magnet. So I don't see how it could inadvertently draw this superweapon and…

Hematite, yes. Really? It means "egg"? Now that is interesting. Very, very interesting.

You have got my attention.

How do you spell that? Oolitic hematite. Half a second, I'm going to write that down. O-O-L-I-T-I-C. And it means egg, egg stone? Goodness. Sedimentary rock, yes, you can see that. It looks different from the main island of Newfoundland, doesn't it? The rock around Portugal Cove is light and dark, gold and grey. Bell Island's red, rising steeply from the sea, tall cliffs. Wonderful soil, here. The coast is very regular, you'll have noticed. Almost no indentations or coves. It's a big egg shape itself. Almost like someone dropped it into Conception Bay from space.

But that's not an uncommon kind of rock here on Earth. You'll find it all over the world. Here, the bottom of the Aral Sea, Egypt, Saudi Arabia, Russia. And China, yes, China has a lot of the stuff.

They opened up the first iron ore mine on Bell Island in the 1890s, a surface mine. That's right, that's why most of us are here at all, the mining. They went down under the ocean, under The Tickle. Conception Bay. It's the biggest submarine iron mine in the whole world. It's as big as St. John's. Have you taken the tour? You should come down on my tour, I'm one of the guides. Yes, I am the oldest Bell Island Mine Museum tour guide. Although Mr. Carter's getting up there. Anyway, come on the tour. I think you'll like it.

We were one of the world's major producers of iron ore. Oh, yes, during the Second World War we had ships anchored here. When I was seven years old, they torpedoed and sank four warships, right there. Look out the window and you can see where they were anchored. Seventy merchant mariners lost their lives. And one torpedo struck the DOSCO iron ore loading dock. The Germans didn't mean to bomb the shore; it was an errant torpedo. But it turned out to be the only location in North American to be subject to a direct attack by German forces during the war. Even if it was a mistake, yes, it was still an attack. The whole island shook.

Where was I?

The Grebe's Nest.

No, I wasn't supposed to be there. I was supposed to be in bed. I wasn't a very good little girl; don't use me as your model. You know what Catherine Aird said: If you can't be a good example, then you'll just have to be a horrible warning. She's an author, mysteries… never mind. Anyway, when the Germans attacked, I was down in the Nest with a headlamp I'd filched from my father, who was a miner, of course; almost everyone on the island worked in the mines back then. I was visiting my eggs.

Oh. The eggs.

I didn't mean to tell you about that.

But really, what's the harm? It's all going to come out sooner rather than later.

What do you think is the real reason two physicists came to visit us here on Bell Island after the Boom? You might know better than I. They were into a particular branch of physics as I recall, something…

Plasma physics, that's right. Something to do with lightning.

Yes, that makes sense; if plasma is electrically conductive, it responds to electromagnetic fields. Infinitely conductive, I see. Really? And it can form filaments and beams?

Could it form a passage?

That's a very interesting idea. Space is filled with it, is it? A network of currents that transfer energy over large distances… I see. The solar wind is plasma. It's the most abundant form of ordinary matter in the Universe?

I think you have just explained something I've been wondering about for a long, long time.

Well, you will think I'm crazy. But you've explained it to me, how they can get from Mars to here. That's been the sticking point for me all along. But if they can ride this solar wind, like a passage…

My eggs. Or what comes out of them, anyway, that's what I'm talking about.

They weren't *my* eggs. I just called them that. Of course I don't lay eggs. What are they teaching—

Down in the nest. The Grebe's Nest.

You can see the layers of iron ore in the cliffs; there are all kinds of fossils. And there's this one place, about ten feet off the beach, that looks like a great big nest full of red eggs.

They're about the size of your head, yes, bigger than an ostrich egg. And they're red like the stone around them. In fact, you could just imagine they were strange egg-shaped formations in the stone, something that got fossilized back when the rock was part of North Africa, five hundred million years ago, and it was on the bottom of the sea.

They were there for anybody to see. I first noticed them during the war. I was only seven years old. But I always had my nose in a book, and I had a lot of ideas, and I noticed something that nobody else seemed to about the stone nest in the cliff.

Snow or ice never stayed on them for long.

I made myself a little tower of flattish rocks so I could climb up and touch the fossils or whatever they were.

The egg things were warm to the touch.

On the surface it looked like a hundred and two of them. Yes, me love, I counted them. I took a real interest in those stones. And when those torpedo attacks occurred, when the island shook, it seemed to me that for a brief moment, that nest of stones sent out a ruddy glow. But that soon disappeared, and afterward, I could never say for certain if it had happened or not.

I used to go down to the beach very often and visit my eggs. Climb down the cliff, down the old cable. This was before they blasted the tunnel, you see. I got a reputation for being odd. As if I wasn't odd enough already for reading books about Mars.

I felt Chosen. The eggs had chosen me.

My dreams changed. My dreams became long, and dark, and full of strange music. I got so that I just loved going to bed, because with my head full of the eggs' humming, I'd dream.

My mother said she'd never seen anything like it. Before, it'd been like pulling teeth to get me to bed. I was the baby of the family, and I guess I always felt like when I went to bed I was missing out. I'd scream and cry when I was a youngster, or worse, I'd sulk. Mother used to say my sulking was like a fog. "You don't have to make a federal case out of it," she used to say. Federal case. Newfoundland was a country back then, its very own country. Oh, you know about that, do you? I am glad they are teaching you something.

But yes, now I loved going into my little room and… sliding down. Not like sleeping. It felt less like dreams, and more like dipping back into one long dream. A long sleep, shared by many minds at once, minds that… communed. I'd feel like my body wasn't my own. It'd stretch, it'd be enormous. Full of energy; *made* of energy. I'd remember soaring through long, lazy strands of ice-blue cloud. Vast, languid beats, great wings made of lightning. Living between and around… this. What we call reality. A red land. Dry. Terrible mountains, and glaciers burning cold. Thin air. Heat, and…

What's that, me son? The eggs?

Well, yes, I kept going down there and reading to the eggs, talking to them, telling them about my life. Sometimes

I'd hum, and it seemed to me that they hummed back. Maybe I imagined it. I was lonely, a lonely little girl, I suppose.

I never told anyone a thing about them. I knew they'd think I was touched. Touched. Nuts, crazy in the head, that's what touched means. But now I'm telling you. I think it's time to tell somebody.

I am quite sane, if old. I've passed all my memory tests. I still have my driver's licence. If that doesn't prove sanity, what does in this society, I ask you.

Next, all the mines were closed. Every mine on Bell Island. There was lots of competition from all over the world, and we'd never made sure that local people owned the mines, that's why. So everybody was all set to leave. There were over twelve thousand people living here then, can you imagine? Now there's only about two thousand of us. I was pretty ancient by that time, the 1960s. I was around thirty or so. And everyone was leaving. My parents left; Dad was about ready to retire anyway, and they went into St. John's; Mother always did like to shop. My brothers left. One to CBS, one to St. John's, two out to Alberta to work in the oil fields.

I stayed. I wasn't married or anything. The eggs took care of that. I didn't have time or inclination for dating or courting or whatever it's called now. I stayed, and got a job here and a job there. Had to commute back and forth on the ferry for a few years because there was no work to be had on the island. I cleaned houses. And I kept visiting the eggs. It was easier, because by then they'd blasted the tunnel.

I'd wake up slowly in those days. I'd have to set my alarm very, very early to be ready for people, for work. Sometimes it'd take me an hour just to stand up and put on my clothes. I couldn't move too fast. My eyes took a long time to adjust, too. Funny things, these human bodies. So small and meaty and chilly.

Then it was 1978.

My dreams went black and cold. It was a whole long dream, a dream that lasted for months before the Boom. It was, I realized slowly, a migration. The dreamer was migrating from the red place, the home place, the dry place, riding the electric wind. The long, black, airless cold, the between, gradually gave way, and the watery world came into focus. Watery world – that's us, the Earth. We have a lot more water than Mars. So.

So, we're coming up to the Boom again now. Goodness, that's like me, I can't seem to help but to tell a story in a spiral.

The Boom, I was down on the beach, and when that bolt hit, the nest just… came apart.

That's right. The eggs, or stones if you want to call them that, fell out onto the beach. Some of them, anyway. There were far more of them than I'd thought. I'd only been able to see the front of the nest, you see, that was the hundred and two I'd counted. But more than that fell out. Far more. And in behind, you could see they went back far, far into a sort of perfectly round, smooth tunnel. I'd say there were thousands, at least. Although without taking them all out it'd be impossible to tell.

The Boom dislodged them, that's right.

I got even more curious, then.

Oh, yes, I took tools to them. Chisels and hammers and everything I had until I broke one, and what came out...

See this scarring across my hand? And the way I can't really close it? That's from what happened. Liquid fire. Magma, maybe. I'm lucky I didn't lose a finger. If I hadn't been wearing gloves...

I scooped up a few of the ones that had fallen out of the nest, all I could carry, to save them from being washed out to sea...

But that's probably enough for your report now, isn't it.

The dream? Well, I'm sure I'm simply foolish.

The dreamer came close, came closer still. The watery planet filled her awareness. And she plunged into the atmosphere, following the filament, the path between our worlds. She plummeted toward Bell Island. I don't know, I just felt it was a she. She came from Mars to awaken the eggs. She impacted the island, and sent a jolt right through the magnetic ore to the nest on the other side. She jolted them free.

The Bell Island Boom came from Mars.

Well, yes, that's an interesting fact, too. Mars is full of hematite. It's one of the most abundant minerals in the rocks and soils there; NASA has proven it. That's why it's so red, red, like Bell Island. They seem to be attracted to hematite, to need it. I don't know how to understand their being. I'm just Susan Fitzgerald who reads too much science fiction and is touched in the head.

Certainly, they must live for a very long time. Thousands of years, maybe. Maybe they never ever die.

Well, of course I have a theory. Here it is. If you look at the stories, it seems like there is a cycle of perhaps six thousand years. Think of all the legends. Chinese, Persian, Slavic, Indian, African, European. Water Serpents. The Leviathan.

Dragons.

They come here to lay their eggs. They hatch here; I think they need water for the first cycle of their lives. And there's lots of prey here. The young need food to thrive. Here, have another cookie.

And then, when they're ready, off they go, back to Mars. Where there's all that nice, red magnetic rock. They are, or become, beings of energy, perhaps. That's what I think. Living plasma, that's a good idea. Sentient energy.

They commute between planets, riding the solar wind. Migrate. Like the wee grebe.

So. Soon the eggs will hatch, and we'll have the first cycle of dragons here on Earth in over six thousand years. And I'll be alive to see it! I hope so, anyway. That will be exciting, won't it?

If we live through it.

I am not sure they worry too much about us. I mean, we're not all that relevant, except as a source of nutrition.

Anyway, thank you for coming and interviewing an old lady, even if she isn't fully a century old.

What? Oh, you noticed that, did you? I didn't finish telling you what I did with the fallen eggs. Very perceptive of you.

Well, to be honest, they're here.

No, not on the cookie plate. They're in a metal trunk, under my bed.

Do you want to see them?

They've gotten hotter than before, and sometimes, they move. Just a little rocking motion. My dreams have gotten longer now. Does the prey dream the dream of the hunter? Soon I'll have to retire, just to keep dreaming.

You're right. That's them, that sound, rattling around in the iron trunk under me bed. Don't worry, it's been happening for months. Do you want to see them? No?

All right, me son. Go catch that next ferry, you'll just be in time.

What an exciting time in history. To be alive to see it!

Where the stars shine out their wonder, and the seas roll up their thunder.

Yes, thank you, glad you enjoyed the cookies. Goodness, can't you run fast?

Goodbye.

Goodbye.

Demoted

It was the last day of second term before things got interesting, an icy April day, wind off the water. The seminar
leader set the discussion: *Is kindness rational?* An ugly boy and
a macho name-dropper debated; Tom looked out the window. The ugly boy – short red cowlicked hair, glasses – said
Hobbes's "warre of alle against alle" was misunderstood,
taken out of historical and cultural context (he was always
saying things like this, annoying the Great-Ideas-Are-
Eternal seminar leader); the name-dropper countered with
Kant and Nietzsche. The redhead responded with
Rousseau, and hitchhiking.

"You always get where you want to go," Massachusetts
farm boy accent coming through. "They'll warn you about
psychos, but someone always picks you up."

Tom had a thing for redheads; the ugliness of this boy
had been a depressant from day one. But now, gaydar
pinged. He spoke to the creature after class.

"You got to believe in kindness." His name was Greeb.
For real; he insisted on it. "How else would you get out of
bed in the morning?"

"From a keen interest in seeing what horror the world
brings forth today."

Greeb laughed. "But see," he said, "people run the world these days as if self-interest is the ruling principle. But it's a *choice*, a mass performance," and he lowered his voice. "The current of kindness – and I mean that in every sense, our deep kinship, yeah? – that current never stops running. Even in the worst places in the world." He put his hand on Tom's forearm, and Tom felt a thrill running up to his shoulder, around and down his spine. "How do you explain that?"

When Greeb said *worst places in the world* Tom knew he meant Darfur, Kabul. But it summoned an image of his own bedroom at home.

"Are you a Christian?"

Meaning *proselytizing fundamentalist*, although given the red hair Tom expected Greeb to be a fellow recovering Catholic. But Greeb laughed and laughed – too hard.

"Hasn't someone ever helped you out for no reason?" He flapped his hands, faggoty. "A guardian angel."

Tom's mother insists: *If you believe in angels, they will come to you.*

Is that a threat, Mom, or a dare?

And then Greeb challenged Tom to a hitchhiking race, Boston to New York. The way he said *New York*, he might as well be saying *Heaven*. "That's right, baby, New York. And if you get there first, I'll trumpet you through the gates."

Tom felt certain Greeb was coming on to him. He was repulsive, but on the other hand he'd be the grateful type. "Why are you taking such an interest in my welfare?"

The sadness in Greeb's eyes was unfathomable. "Me and my whole family, we are charged with a mission: to try to do good."

"Your family has a mission statement?"

Tom was laughing, but Greeb nodded, solemn. Tom thought how he'd never noticed before how very green Greeb's eyes were.

"What's the point?"

"In doing good?"

"Yeah." Tom made his voice hard. "In a world as horrible as this one – with people as horrible as me in it – what's some little drop of kindness going to do?"

Greeb didn't answer, and so Tom's words hung between them. He felt the truth of them, ringing in the air; he was intimate with the extent of his own misanthropy. And saying it like that, to this green-eyed creature, made it all just a little more true: another nail in the coffin of brotherly love. In Tom something writhed: inchoate longing, drowning in cynicism.

Tom broke the silence.

"And what makes you think I need your do-gooding?"

"It's obvious." Greeb flapped his fingers as if he could climb air. "You're like me. You want to *ascend*."

Tom's mother wanted to pay for a cell phone.

He'd made the mistake of calling to tell her about his end-of-term adventure. Tom could picture her huddling in the dingy Gardner kitchen, landline receiver cradled between ear and shoulder; she'd catch it from his father if he caught her babying their son. *If the little fucker won't get a job then he doesn't get a phone/new sneakers/a car*. She offered, he refused, her voice started shaking. She was probably clutching at the cross on the gold chain around her throat. "You will come back, right? Finish up the degree?"

"What do you think."

"Tom. Was it… Did the Father ever… do anything to you?"

It being the unspoken, terrible thing that was *wrong* with Tom. But the idea of Father Clancy "doing" anything… disgusting. He would never tell her about his first redhead. Billy was nasty but gorgeous, creepy and beautiful as an angel should be. *Angel* equalled physical pain, pleasure, confusion, social humiliation (adept bully, Billy); also the room in the church basement, choir robes, skin. Everything in black and white except the ruddy glow of Billy's hair.

"Why New York?" Her voice choked like she was saying *Sodom*.

He refused to respond. When her crying became audible, he hung up.

Tom stood at the intersection of Tremont and Marginal Road, thumb out, hoping for a ride onto the I-90 West. His sneakers had holes, his jacket was inadequate, it was foggy. Cars sped by, one guy deliberately swerving to splash Tom with polluted water. He thought of giving it up, then pictured his father's derision. *Fuckin' loser can't even catch a ride out of Boston. Little fairy.*

And then a white car pulled over.

Tom froze, staring; then lurched forward. A woman, baby asleep in a car seat in the back.

"Where you headed?"

"New York."

Perfect.

The woman had short hair. She wore a white Bench sweater, pilling and a stain down the front. Fortyish. Eyes as green as Greeb's; must be wearing those coloured contacts, colour so vivid it looked fake.

"My name's Glee, by the way."

"I'm Tom. That yours?" Tom jerked his head at the sleeping kid.

"Yes." That tender mom-look spread over her face. "I call her Geek."

How sweet.

She had broken up with her husband she said. Tom hoped she wouldn't go on about this. She rambled a bit about how she'd had second thoughts. She still loved him, she said. She was going to intersect him on the road. "All we have is each other," she said, "since we were shut out."

Shut out of what? Tom stayed quiet and at last so did she.

They got out onto the interstate, into what would have been a sunset on a better day. Tom watched the outskirts of the city spin by: new leaves on trees, churches, the ugliness of a mall. Tom dozed with his head against the window.

He was back in Gardner High, the day things slipped. Between classes, a shove in the hallway, *Bitch*. Nothing new, but Tom turned on the jock with his chemistry textbook. The feeling of his body coming around, the follow-through with the book. Wanting, in that moment, to sever the jock's head from his body. Knocked him to the floor and the guy even lost consciousness for a moment.

Tom felt he was falling, came to. It was now entirely dark; the car slid over the road and oncoming headlights swooped and passed.

"Nice snooze?"

Tom rubbed his face with his hand. "Nightmare, actually."

"You were whimpering."

He stared at the blankness out the window, willing her not to talk. They'd pulled him from school, sent him for counseling. The doctor told his mother it was the stress of coming out. Her face opening, wounded. She'd had no fucking idea.

Tom had finished high school from home; his mother rewarded him by paying for college. She thought he was too fragile to get a job.

A flare of light from the woman's face jerked his attention around. "Want a smoke?"

"Do you think we should?" Tom indicated the kid in back.

"She started it."

He looked behind. A face in the dark, lit with dim fire, blew smoke in his face. What he'd thought was a toddler was a sullen-faced teen. Tom turned away, the world tilting.

Wordlessly, he accepted the smoke.

"We're getting there," Glee said. "Soon we can stretch our wings."

"Good." The girl yawned. There was a rustling sound like the car seat was packed with paper. "He coming with us?"

"Tom?" the woman asked. "Are you coming with us?"

"To New York? Yeah, that's where we're going, right?" Tom looked out the window. "This isn't the interstate."

"I decided to take the back roads. So much prettier."

"Mom, can I bite him?" The girl's eyes were as green as her mother's.

"No."

"Oh. Please?"

"Geek…" in that mom-warning tone.

"God bless, then, Tom or whatever your name is." The girl wriggled her shoulders. That rustling again; it made Tom's skin crawl.

"Yes, God bless. God bless us all." Glee looked sad. "As we wait here on earth for Heaven to open its gates once more."

Tom made a decision.

"Um, you can just let me out here."

"But it's raining." The windshield was dotted with water.

"No, really. It's okay." Tom put his hand on the door handle, raised his voice. "Let me out."

The woman sighed. "All right." She slowed. "Come with us. We're just demoted, that's all. Please?"

"No, thanks."

Tom couldn't get out of the car fast enough.

It didn't take long for the red eyes of taillights to disappear.

Rain spit out of the sky.

No traffic, nothing, dark. Soon he was shivering, rain trickling through thin spiked hair.

Later found him sitting on his backpack, shuddering with cold. He'd given up trying to look normal and had wrapped a T-shirt around his head.

No way of knowing the time.

Maybe he slept.

He came to, stiff and miserable. Light leaking into the sky. Not one single car had come by all night.

He wondered where Greeb was – probably halfway to New York. *Guardian angels*. Idiot. Kindness – Greeb's Holy Grail – was just another cover for self-interest. People were nice to get laid, or get money, or be liked because that led to getting laid or money.

Mom tries to be kind, the thought came. No. Her martyred attempts to get him to behave, so she didn't look like a bad mother, weren't kindness. He shut his heart against her tears, her furtive attempts to bribe him into loving her.

As for his father...

Lights down the road.

Tom pulled the T-shirt from his head and stood up. He stuck his arm out, thumb rising high.

The car sped by.

Still, it had been a car. Light grew, revealing the shitty roadscape. Strip malls on either side, closed down. Empty farmers' fields. Trees. The woman had dropped him on the moon.

Cars went by. No one stopped. Tom ate his three granola bars, wanted coffee so bad he thought he'd throw up. The monotony of the landscape was a nightmare, or waves of pain. Closed, peeling strip malls. Fragmented forest. Abandoned fields.

New York – the fantasy of making out with a guy he'd never seen before, of not being the faggot who lost his shit in high school (yeah, that story had followed him to Boston, thanks to Gardner High's graduating class of 2012) – was enough to keep his hand unfolding like a machine with every passing car. His feet in their crappy sneakers hurt. It was intolerably boring. It got dark.

Rain began again, driving into his face. He wrapped the T-shirt around his head, kept walking. Of course no one picked him up; it was some curse that warned people off, something wrong with him. That, and the world was fucked. No one was *kind*. Kin. Kinship. *Someone always picks you up.*

When he'd accepted the bet, Tom had asked, *Do I have to believe in your kindness theory?*

Greeb's eerie, green eyes had looked grave behind his glasses. *Why would you accept a bet if you don't believe in the terms?*

I just don't believe people pick you up out of kindness.

But he wanted to get out of friggin' Massachusetts. *Ascend.* This wasn't philosophical. He wanted a warm car ride off this fucking moon.

Rubber legs, God, was it never going to end? The shoulder crumbled into peaty brownness, but he kept on. One foot in front of the other.

Headlights, a roar behind him. He didn't bother turning around. Light grew and his shadow lengthened and danced. Then the squeal of brakes and it was a dragon's breath, close, hot, hot and huge and hard, lifting him up from behind and he was flying.

Tom hurt. Jerked around like a giant dog had him in its jaws. AC/DC blaring, smoke and sulphur, red and orange light. A dashboard, him slumped against metal. Burgundy velour seats, door handle missing.

"Jesus, I thought you was a goner there." Driver a giant, taking up half the cab. "I thought you was dead!" Tom tried to sit up; pain ripped through him and he screamed. "Broke your arm there, blood on your head. Jesus, Mary, I thought you was a goner!"

Camouflage hat, jacket, pants, the red cheeks and blonde eyelashes of a redhead; clenched his cigarette so hard that it looked like he'd bite it off.

"I'm taking you to a hospital."

Tom managed to say, "Boston."

"Providence. I'm in the army. Yeah, just visiting family." The man threw his butt on the floor, lit another. "Girls won't look at you if you're in the army. Not a fucking glance. Wife dumped me. By *text*. While I was in *Afghanistan*. Fucking bitch. Know what I mean? Know what I mean? Bitches. You're not a faggot, are you?"

The truck jolted; Tom bit back another scream.

"Don't worry, I got nothing against little faggots. My little brother's one. We got nothing in common but the green eyes and the wings." The man laughed. "Thought I'd hit a dog back there. I was just going to drive on but then I saw you in the headlights of an oncoming car. Also, I had a witness, didn't I? Had to pick you up! My name's Gormless, by the way."

Gormless? And that red hair... "Is your little brother named Greeb?"

"They'll fix you up good in Providence. Stop trying to move, don't be fucking stupid."

The pain then got so bad that Tom threw up. That was the last thing he remembered for a while.

Elbow broken; his funny bone. Concussion. The humiliating phone call to his mother to see if the medical insurance still covered him. Strange that his back wasn't injured where the truck hit him; he tried to tell them, but no one would listen. They put him under, wired his bones, stapled the skin like Bride of Frankenstein. Nausea that wouldn't go away; they shoved a needle of Gravol into his thigh.

They kept him a few days.

A doctor offered to take him back to Gardner. "If that's where you're going." High and pleasant voice.

"Sure," Tom said. No New York now. The doctor had goddamn green eyes, it was a pandemic around here. But Tom accepted the offer.

He limped out into the parking lot, sky spread overhead like a warning. He had a nice ass, the doctor. A pickup truck, much shinier than that of the crazed army man. Tom climbed inside; everything was harder with one arm.

"So that guy who brought you in, that was pretty nice of him."

"That guy? Nice? He hit me on the road."

"What?"

"I said," Tom enunciated, "he hit me. Only took me into the hospital because he thought someone witnessed the accident."

The doctor drove on in silence. "Mind if I smoke?"

This surprised Tom. "Go ahead."

The doctor lit up. "There was no evidence of that kind of trauma."

"What?" it was Tom's turn to say.

"I said, there was no evidence of that kind of trauma."

The doctor thought he was lying or crazy. "He hit my backpack, sent me flying," Tom almost yelled.

"Sure."

Silence.

"You live in Providence?" Tom asked.

"I wish. No. Go to Boston to party sometimes."

He flashed a glance and suddenly Tom saw it, soft-hard look in the guy's eyes.

"You?" the doctor said.

"What?"

"You party much?"

The doctor was looking right at him now, not at the road; shifting in his seat as he drove, spreading his legs. He was coming on to Tom, here, in this truck. Tom's heart beat faster. "Sometimes," he said.

The doctor was bigger than he'd thought, his shoulders took up half the cab. He'd given Tom a ride for this, for sex of course. Not "kindness." *Wrong again, Greeb,* Tom thought. "Sometimes."

The doctor laughed, deep and loud, butching out or something; okay, Tom could deal.

"I thought you were a goner," the doctor said.

"On the operating table?"

"You like danger?"

Danger? Fear and excitement coiled in the pit of Tom's stomach. "I've had enough danger for one lifetime."

The man laughed again. He shifted his shoulders, scratching his back against the seat; a papery rustling filled the cab. Tom shrank back against the passenger door, cradling his aching arm. "You like boxing?"

"No." Maybe this guy was a psycho. He should've called his mom from the hospital; she'd come out to get him, Christ, even his old man would've sprung him.

"You know what I love? The way they fall into each other's arms at the end of the round."

"Sure."

"It's like when I cut someone open. It's intimate. Visceral, you know? You ever hunted? You ever killed anyone?"

"No."

"You use email?"

"Of course."

"Use email or texting rather than talk on a phone?"

"Sometimes." Was this a test?

"How about meeting someone? You ever choose to actually meet someone rather than being their Facebook fucking friend?"

"Of course."

"You know what's wrong with this world?"

"What?"

"Everyone's in full retreat!"

"Sure."

"Don't just say *sure*, are you even listening?"

This fucker was like his old man, wanting to expound and humiliate. "Back off, okay?" Tom yelled. "Back off!"

The man threw his cigarette onto the floor, lit another. "That's the spirit."

Get me home, Tom prayed. He hated home. Just get me home.

"We're engaged in a mass performance."

Greeb had said that. Hadn't Greeb said that? Tom stared out the windshield. "Mass performance of what?"

"What do you think?"

What had Greeb said? "Of self-interest."

"No!" the man exploded. "The performance is a mass retreat from the visceral! From physicality, from the incomprehensibility of physicality!"

The man was crazy.

"My wife broke up with me by text," he went on. "Didn't even phone me."

"Your... wife?" Tom faltered.

"While I was on my last tour of duty in Afghanistan. Fucking bitch."

A scream broke from Tom; he clutched at the door but the handle was torn off. "Let me out of here, just stop and let me out!"

"Okay, calm down now." The man slowed. Someone, a girl, stood by the highway, hoodie up. She was smoking, hip jutted, insolent. "My daughter," the man said to Tom.

It was that kid, the kid from the car. Green eyes, they all had green eyes and pointed teeth.

Tom flailed at the seatbelt one-handed.

The man parked by the girl and peeled himself from the pickup. Wings, like a giant dragonfly's, down his back.

"How's your mother?" he asked the girl.

"Good. As usual." The girl pouted. "She's on her way."

The man opened the passenger door for Tom. "You don't have to do this, you know. Just accept the ride."

"Fuck you." Tom stumbled from the truck.

The girl, Glee, stared. She spread her double set of gossamer wings, scattering light, rustling in the breeze. "You didn't get very far."

A noise came from the back of the truck. Tom turned to see Greeb, emerging tousled from under a tarp.

"Hi." Greeb smiled at Tom. "Want a ride?"

Tom tried to back away, tangled one foot behind the other and fell on his ass.

"That's my brother," the big man said, tender, tired, proud. "My baby brother. He's the best of us. He keeps an eye on the gates, and one day they will open to us again and we will ascend."

"Greeb." The girl jerked her head at Tom. "Are you an idiot? Why didn't you tell him about the terms?"

Greeb's smile died. "Of course I told him. But he doesn't believe in kindness."

"You can't agree to a bet if you don't believe in the terms," the girl said to Tom. "You're stuck."

"Get the fuck away," Tom whispered.

A humming came out of the sky. Something that looked like a beam of light pierced the greyness; it resolved itself into a woman, the older woman, his first ride. She landed softly in the back of the truck, folding her wings along her back. Greeb's face lit up, and he shrank until he was a little winged baby. The woman took him in her arms.

The vast winged man spoke. "Taking me back, Baby?"

"Of course, Gorm." She shifted her eyes to Tom. "Hello, Tom."

"He's not coming," Gormless said.

"Dad scared the poor little shit," the girl explained.

The woman's green eyes were full of kindness. "It's not Dad's fault. Tom's not ready."

All of them, even the rust-downed baby, shook their heads.

The man and girl got into the truck. It was an awkward fit with wings, but after some adjustments they folded the gossamer appendages along their backs and settled in. The man brought the truck around in a tight U-turn.

They drove away, toward the place where they hoped they'd find heaven.

Tom could see the woman's face as she sat swaying in the cargo bed – Greeb in her arms – her sad, kind, green eyes on him. The truck getting smaller and smaller, shrinking on the endless highway. Gone.

No cars, wind moaning.

Peeling, abandoned strip malls, empty fields. Alone and waiting.

Tom stared in the direction that the truck had gone. Tire tracks along the pavement, still visible, into the distance.

Something itched between his shoulder blades, something pushing under the skin.

Tom walked onto the road in his holey sneakers. He lined himself up, feet in the tire tracks. He bounced a little, feeling his toes, the spring in his feet. And Tom began to run.

Show and Tell

I came late to the dance. I arrived hoping Marnie would already be there. I'd almost asked her if she wanted to go together, but I'd said nothing and now, I arrived alone.

The building still left me feeling queasy; it smelled the same. The interior walls were painted cinder blocks, glossed in brighter colours than in my day. But the school office looked the same. I remembered being sent there to get the strap for daydreaming, after being warned to pay attention three times, like in a fairy tale. Here on the island, back in the '70s in any case, there were penalties for fantasy; or maybe it was just that the teacher disliked me in particular, so very much.

But that was then. Now, twenty years later, I could hear music pumping from the gym and I saw the flash of colours; someone had rented a disco ball. I heard laughter, adult laughter. That was nice, right? Different. This was different.

I went into the gym and moved directly to the special-event licensed table, bought a beer, and surveyed the room. I'd had a sick feeling that some of my old classmates might show up this night, come back to... I don't know. Torture me. I gave myself a mental shake. I hadn't seen any of them in almost two decades. They had no way of knowing that I was even here.

This, my old elementary school, had been slated for demolition, an event I anticipated with dark and vengeful pleasure. In the interim, some enterprising spark had arranged for the building to be rented out to community groups for special events, and here we were, the fundraising committee for the dragon boat team, dancing at the seventies-themed fundraiser and, well, raising funds. Joining the team was how I'd met Marnie. She was the steerer, and fierce, yelling instructions from her adaptive seat in the stern. Also, Marnie was gay, although she and I had never talked about this.

I looked for her now, some beer safely inside me. She wasn't hard to spot. She'd found patch-pocket flares, a groovy open-necked shirt, and rainbow socks with toes. She'd decorated her wheelchair with those plastic straw things we used to put on our bicycle wheels so they made a vaguely musical noise. She was out on the dance floor, carving it up.

I drank the beer too fast and joined her. I admired her rainbow-toed socks. After two dances – to "Dancing Queen" and the song from the Star Wars cantina – Stevie Wonder came on. "Sir Duke."

"Sometimes I feel like I'm living the wrong life."

That just came out of me. Things like that happen sometimes. I immediately regretted saying it, but it was too late.

"It's because we're in your old school, isn't it?"

Which made me smile. Marnie knew me well enough at this point to grasp that my thoughts were usually only tenuously related to external stimulus; the thought was something I generated myself, out of the spastic weirdness of my own brain. Suddenly I didn't feel like talking about wrong lives anymore. "Never mind."

Marnie, I'd learned over the past month, hated *never minds* beyond all things, and teased me and poked at me until I elaborated. And indeed, part of me may have begun and then feebly tried to end the conversation on purpose. Because there was something *about* having Marnie pay attention to me.

"That there's some other life that's supposed to be yours," I yelled over Stevie, "but you've taken a wrong turn and the life you're supposed to be living is going on without you. The conscious *here* you."

"The conscious here me?" She executed a nifty spin in her chair.

"The you that, in this particular narrative, drags on, making the best of it, but... it isn't your life."

"But if you're here, then it's your life." She was taking this seriously. "Multiple universes?"

I kept dancing.

"Maybe it's not about universes," she proposed. "Maybe it's a narrative, like you said. Maybe it's what you choose to remember."

Which was pretty perceptive, because I had difficulty remembering all kinds of things.

The song after Stevie was "Don't Give Up on Us," slow. I got self-conscious and left Marnie to go get another beer. Got trapped by the guy who helped organize everything: he'd lost his wife to cancer and seemed determined to talk to me. All the time. "Why don't you like Santok?" Marnie had demanded, because really, Santok was nice and good looking and his wife had been gone for five years so it wasn't creepy or anything.

I didn't tell Marnie that I'd never really dated. Just had sex. Not even good sex. I didn't tell her that I hated sex, but I seemed to want to have it all the time, with men I didn't like who didn't like me. I didn't tell her, or Santok, that I was trying not to do that anymore.

So I extricated myself from the nice, flirtatious, Marnie-approved man, and that's when I decided to take a walk around my old elementary school. Before it was consigned to dust forever, damn it to hell.

Walking down the darkened hallway, I realized my face was stretched in a weird, teeth-baring grimace. I gave my cheek a slap, trying for a reset. My mainlander grandmother used to whack the back of my hand every time I made a face: scrunch up my nose, for example, or purse my lips. Crossing my eyes, encouraged in my brothers as amusing, was of course forbidden. Let's not even bring up sticking out my tongue. She didn't tell me that if the wind changed, my face would stick that way, which is what my Newfoundland relatives all said. My mainland grandmother said it was "unattractive."

I wasn't a little girl who understood "attractive" except that I suspected I wasn't.

And neither was Saucy Doll. But I wanted her, and so did thousands of other little girls. Saucy Doll had a glamour on her, some kind of power. The ads made her seem like someone fun, companionable. Someone who could change things.

And she was ugly. Innocuously ugly, with blue eyes and blonde hair before Karla Homolka sinisterized blue eyes and blonde hair, and even she hasn't, in the end, succeeded. A pink dress, with a gingham undershirt. Her go-to expression was eyes wide, lips parted in that semi-pornographic expression female dolls often model. But the whole point of her was this: you would take her left arm and pump it up and down, and as you did so, her face would change.

Saucy Doll had several expressions. You had to go through them all, in the same order every time. The arm didn't move smoothly – it made a rattling, mechanical noise with every pump. Eyes rolled to the left, lips parted even further. A faintly alarming creaking noise as the semi-flexible rubber of her face stretched, the mechanism beneath just faintly perceptible. Then there'd be a sort of click, and her lips would snap closed as her eyes moved to the right.

When that one was done, she'd snap back to her original position, blue eyes staring straight into mine. Next, she'd wink her right eye. Her left cheek would begin to hitch up; after her right eye snapped back open (and it never went back up all the way, just stayed partly closed with her improbably black eyelashes curling up, lending her an eerie resemblance – one I recognized even then – to my mother after one too many evening ryes) the left eye would begin to close, and the hitch of the cheek continued, so that by the time she winked with her left eye she looked demented. It was a relief when that one returned to normal.

Her next trick was a sort of proto yawn, with eyes closed (usually they didn't close simultaneously; we're talking serious Uncanny Valley here). Then her eyes hitched to the left, and her lips compressed. Jowls appeared, and a sort of uh-oh-what-have-I-done expression. But she snapped out of that and back to happy-neutral pretty quick, closed her eyes, and smiled. That expression reminded me of pictures of saints, usually just as they were about to die.

Her eyes would then pop open, and be crossed.

That was the last expression and, of course, my favourite. Then the cycle began again, with several awkward, stiff pumps of her arm. There was an unescapably jerky, masturbatory quality to the action.

I knew that because I'd seen the boy next door masturbate. Bob was vastly old, thirteen. About a week after Saucy came into my life he got me to take off my pants, and show him my places, and after we'd gone through this a few times he asked me if I wanted to see his.

I didn't, but I didn't say so.

And that's when I saw this masturbation thing for the first time.

Before these incidents, I'd been an enthusiastic little masturbator myself, although I didn't know that's what I was doing. I'd straddle my spool-carved, maple bed's footboard and ride it until my hair was damp with sweat. I had an image in my mind of a big field full of beautiful, giant flowers. The flowers opened and opened and opened, under a beautiful, soft blue sky.

I stopped that after the boy next door started looking at my parts. I didn't like riding any more. And after seeing him masturbate I stopped remembering that I'd ever done anything like ride the bed or think of flowers.

I told my mother what had happened with Bob, and she said not to tell anybody, especially my father, and to stop playing with Bob. So, next time Bob asked me to play with him I said I was busy. Playing with dolls was better.

Soon after, Saucy's face grew stiffer. It became harder to make her change. And one of the cats got at her and left bite marks all over her soft, rubbery face. Her hair grew matted, and her dress became grubby. I will never know what possessed me to bring her to Grade One Show and Tell.

Maybe it was because I always forgot. The very first Show and Tell day, I was alerted to the fact too late, after my father had already delivered me, terribly early, on his way to work – just like he did every morning, and I'd stand around in the rain or cold or sun or whatever, because in those days teachers kept the school barricaded against all children until ten minutes to nine – so there I was watching all the other kids arrive, and all of them carried toys, including the horrible spectacle of Jessica, the rich girl, whose rapaciousness was legendary, with a stuffed panda bigger than she was. I felt literally sick. I'd forgotten Show and Tell day. Jessica had a giant, fucking *panda*. And then my scrabbling mind remembered that I was wearing my ring. I wore it every day – my mainland grandparents had given it to me. So, that day, I showed the ring. It wasn't a giant panda, but it was something.

The second time I forgot Show and Tell (I want to say it was every Wednesday, but I'd be making that up), I tried the ring trick again.

"You already showed and told that," Jessica said.

"Yeah," said Monty, and I felt betrayed, because I'd thought Monty was my friend.

"I forgot," I mumbled, and sat back down, face hot and red.

Maybe I brought Saucy that third Show and Tell because she happened to be near the door as my father hustled me out to the car, and I happened to remember. It seems unlikely. There was no earthly reason I'd ever remember Show and Tell. I had trouble remembering that kind of thing, and my parents weren't into remembering for me. Maybe she wanted to go to school with me and somehow planted the suggestion in my mind, although telepathy wasn't one of her powers that I was aware of.

In any case, she came with me and I showed her.

"What happened to her face?" Monty, faithless friend, pointed at Saucy's mutilated visage.

"My cat," I whispered.

"She's ugly!" Jessica jeered. This week, she'd brought a doll almost as tall as me, with white-blonde hair, a red dress trimmed with silver lace, and a rhinestone necklace.

"Saucy Doll! I have one of those!" screeched Heather Two (there were four Heathers in our class and three Cathys).

"So do I, and so does my cousin!" shrieked Cathy Three.

"Yes, Heather, Jessica, Monty, Cathy, we let every person have their show and tell and we don't interrupt them," said the teacher.

It shook me a bit that Heather Two and Cathy Three and Cathy Three's cousin had one. I'd thought I was the only person in all of Newfoundland with a Saucy Doll. But hey, I was up in front of forty-five beady-eyed kids and I'd better show and tell.

It went very well because of the faces. Everyone really liked the last one, the cross-eyed one, and because I was so nervous and wrenched Saucy through them at breakneck speed, everyone insisted that I do it all a second time, and when I was done it raised a general cheer.

I realized the second time around that I went through the faces myself as Saucy did them. Weird. Luckily nobody could see that because I kept my head down.

And luckily nobody noticed that I didn't tell the story of how I got Saucy. That was because I couldn't remember. She'd just appeared in my life. I had no memory of opening a box and finding her, no memory of a parent or grandparent making some comment about her, or a brother trying to steal her or write on her face with a marker. Only the cat seemed to have noticed her.

She'd just appeared; she was not and then she was in my life. Kind of how she showed up at school for Show and Tell.

But maybe there was no real mystery to it. Like I said, I had trouble remembering all kinds of things. I forgot, then, to bring her home. She lived in my classroom cubby hole for weeks. Occasionally, at recess or lunch, I'd reach in and pump her arm, taking her through her paces. She got even stiffer. Her right eye was permanently half-closed, despite attempts at dolly physio, my fruitless nudging of it with a finger.

Finally one day she just stuck, in a terrible no-expression expression, in between.

I shoved her behind a bunch of stuff and forgot her.

Things kept going downhill after that. Suffice it to say that Monty's defection was just the beginning; soon, anybody who'd ever been nice to me or even just tolerated my presence at school turned on me.

Every now and again, at recess, a crowd of girls would form and take me to the bathroom where they made me stick my head in a toilet and lick the water like a dog, while Jessica and all of the Heathers and two of the Cathys looked on. That lasted for the rest of Grade One and most of Grade Two, when it fell out of fashion and, instead, I spent my recesses watching them eat my lunch. They made requests. If I didn't come with what they wanted they'd kick and slap me. It was hard to procure store-bought stuff because my parents didn't give me money for that kind of thing. I became adept at stealing small amounts of change. And my grades dropped because I was hungry. So that was recess.

At lunchtime people mostly just left me alone. It was a relief. I'd read. I had little else to do, my lunch having already been consumed by the others.

In Grade Six Monty shoved me into the boys' bathroom and made me suck his dick.

But Grade Six isn't forever. Right?

Twenty years later here I was, back at what had been my school, fundraising for breast cancer research. Twenty years of my life felt as small and far away as a foreign city viewed through the small end of a telescope. Finishing school, university in Toronto, various arts admin jobs that I never liked as well as I should have, a string of liaisons with people I never cared about as much as I should have. My mother's breast cancer diagnosis. Flying back home on the negative momentum of a job contract ending and the demise of yet another bad-boyfriend "relationship." And then my mother died. It gutted me.

I joined the dragon boat team, I came to the dance, and now here I was, walking down a dark hallway, the sound of merriment fading behind me. I had never been in the building at night before. It gave the whole place a hallucinatory quality, like the midpoint in a horror movie.

I started at the Grade Six end of the building, and worked my way down the hall, peering through the windows of the classroom doors. Grade Six, Grade Five, Grade Four, all in a row. They had a room, empty now, labelled LIBRARY. That was an improvement; when I'd gone to school there, we'd had only a pitiful selection of books in each individual classroom.

There was a drinking fountain, weirdly low on the wall. Right. We'd been shorter.

Past the entrance to the gym. "Car Wash," disco lights flashing warm into the empty hallway. I heard Marnie and the others laughing and shrieking. Three more classrooms to go. Grade Two, then Grade Three, which had always, weirdly, been out of sequence. The horrible desks had been replaced by tables and detachable chairs. Evidently class sizes had diminished – well, of course they had; that's one of the reasons this place was getting torn down. No children anymore, like some child-collecting Pied Piper had drained our entire society.

It was the work of a moment to approach the door of my Grade One classroom, grasp the knob, find it unlocked, and walk inside.

It looked the same. Same desks, with chairs attached. The room was crammed full of them, just as in my day when there were over forty of us in one class. This room, unlike the others, hadn't been updated.

There was a lesson still on the board: math. Additions and subtractions.

At the back still ranged the row of hooks for our coats, and stacks of cubby holes where we'd stash our lunches and such every day.

My cubbyhole had been the one on the bottom around the corner. A mobile chalkboard had been shoved across it; I pulled it out, dislodging a warren-worth of dust bunnies, got down on my knees, and peered into the darkness of the cubby.

It was full, and I took each item out, holding it up to the faint pulsing disco light to see: two textbooks, a pencil, a sweater and a pair of pink socks just the right size for an undersized girl around age six, some discarded lunch bags, an apple that had seen better days, a yellow mitten. I remembered that mitten. My aunt had knit me the pair and I'd promptly lost one, and felt so guilty that I'd kept the survivor in the cubby, where it tortured my conscience every time I looked at it.

I dug around some more. A book I'd brought from home: *Where the Wild Things Are.* Loved that book. The wrappers to a Flakie and a Butterfinger: plunder for the other kids.

At the very back, something hard and round, the size of a large grapefruit, with something attached to it that felt like a Brillo pad. I hauled on it and the other stuff shifted and slid.

Saucy's head, followed by her body.

Even in the shuddering light from down the hall I could see how ugly she was. Her arm was raised in a left-handed Heil Hitler salute and there was dirt smeared across her pocked face. Right eye half-closed, mouth tense in the beginning of some kind of grimace.

I took her hand and pumped her arm, knowing she was broken, but what the hell.

Her face moved! Twenty years of neglect had returned the powers of movement to Saucy.

Some part of my brain was, of course, trying to deal with the utter impossibility of this cubby being full of my stuff, and an apple that had seen better days but not *over twenty years* of better days. But most of me wasn't. Most of me was looking at Saucy and her weird, wide, preternaturally blue eyes.

Look left. Look right. Wink right. Wink left, and grimace. Yawn, look left, uh-oh-what-have-I-done? Happy-neutral-pretty. Closed eyes: saint. Pop open: crossed eyes.

I almost laughed.

I took her through the sequence again.

When I got to the yawn, I yawned too. And then remembered how I'd realized that day at Show and Tell, the day before everything got even worse, that I mirrored Saucy's face when she went through her sequence. And I was doing it again now, and I hadn't even noticed. I mirrored the doll, or did the doll mirror me? On what sick cellular level were Saucy and I communing?

The song in the gym had changed to "Tonight's the Night." Rod Stewart's hoarse voice rang down the hall, singing the creepy, happy lyrics.

I pumped Saucy's arm in time to the music. Might as well go through it again. Third time's the charm, as Gandalf said.

As our eyes rolled to the left, the room flooded with light.

And I remembered the spool bed. Remembered riding it. Man, I used to ride that thing. Kid pleasure, nothing attached to it, no outcomes, no shame, except I suppose I knew not to do it in front of anybody. How could I have forgotten that?

Mechanically, I kept the doll's arm in motion. Her mouth clicked, my lips snapped closer together. The light died, and the music got quieter as well. It wasn't "Tonight's the Night." It was Supertramp. Strange to change a song in the middle like that.

The doll's eyes moved right, and so did mine. When they got so far over that it felt like they'd spin around inside my head, there was another flash of light from down the hall and the Supertramp morphed into slidey guitar and harp, an organ, swelling strings. "Tonight's the Night."

I laughed. And remembered flowers: huge, house-sized flowers, opening and opening and opening in an endless vista of unfolding beauty. Pleasure, pleasure, pleasure, on and on as far as the eye could see or the body experience. Falling through pleasure.

Snap.

Saucy stared straight into my eyes. The music dimmed, morphed, was not what I'd thought.

The wink came next, right eye. I knew it. I kept going.

Wink.

Light.

Tonight's the night.

Cathy One had been nice to me. That's right. Nice. She'd been the one to tell the others to stop making me drink the toilet water. That it made them disgusting pigs. She was fearless; she didn't care that they might turn on her. And what's weirder, they *had* stopped. Moved on to the lunches, but whatever.

Snap. Silence. The school was dark now, no music, no disco light, no laughter. I was crouched in the classroom, alone. And I knew that I was truly, profoundly alone. The world had stopped turning. I felt certain that if I put the doll down and went to the gym, now, there'd be nobody there. All would be dark. And if I went out in the world, nobody would be there either. It'd be the seventies again, my childhood, but empty, dark. Between.

I hung onto the doll's damn arm and pumped it. I did not need to see her; I knew the sequence, could hear her creaking as the skin on her damaged face squeezed, morphed, our cheeks hitching up, right eye opening, left eye closing, that demented wink, the one I hated…

Light, music, tonight's the night. I remembered in Grade Six getting Monty to fuck off with the lunchtime penis-sucking in the boys' washroom. He'd made me do it by threatening me with something, something I couldn't remember. But it had terrified me. Something… telling something he knew about me. Whatever, I couldn't remember. But if I'd just do something for him…and it went on for a while. Maybe a month? I couldn't remember. A month is a long time when you're eleven. And finally I'd gotten him to fuck off with…or had I? It had stopped?

Snap.

Silence.

Creak, creak went the arm.

Yawn.

I yawned right along with the doll, invisible in the darkness.

Tonight's the night.

My ears popped; light flooded the room.

Cathy One and I, kissing. That's what Monty had threatened to tell. That Cathy One and I were dykes. She'd felt so good to kiss, soft, like something, like nibbling something, like flowers. She'd had breasts already, and she not only let me touch them, she wanted me to touch them.

I stayed there for a time, letting that memory wash through me, to Rod Stewart's scratchy voice. Memory, I call it, although it felt like some kind of braided déjà vu. There was a life, my life, where I'd never kissed Cathy One and Monty hadn't had to threaten me with anything. No, I'd just been so scared and checked out and unprotected that anyone could make me do anything. And there was another life where he'd threatened me and I'd crumbled. And another where…

Snap.

Uh-oh-what-have-I-done expression. Ugly, ugly doll. Ugly face, one I'd always hated so much I loved it. It fascinated me. Compressing lips, tight, tighter, edges of mouth turning down, eyes looking left, looking wide.

What you have done, Saucy, is pull my life into tonight's the night. There was another story now, déjà vu, already seen, one where I told Monty to fuck off and then he'd grabbed my hair and smashed my head off the sink. My head had rung and there'd been stars, but I'd twisted around and punched him in the balls, hard, really hard, three times, until he'd let go of my hair and folded onto the floor, staring at me, hands between his legs.

"Touch me again and I'll cut it off," and I'd walked backwards out of the boys' bathroom door, and I'd never had to go in there again.

"She's crazy," Monty had told everybody but I didn't care, because Cathy One and I were friends, forever.

Snap.

Saint.

The next face was saint.

She'd died. I didn't want this thing, this memory or, or whatever it was. Bullshit story, alternate universe, whatever anyone wanted to call it. All gay people have to have tragic lives or something? Bullshit. But it wouldn't go away, tonight's the night. She'd died, something, what? Car accident, that was it. Her family had had an open casket and my mother had brought me to the funeral and said, "You don't have to look." I could tell she was disturbed, thought Cathy One's family must be crazy, but I'd understood why when I saw Cathy's mother standing by the coffin, stroking and stroking Cathy's hair. It was so you'd understand that she was truly dead.

Didn't really look like Cathy. Cathy never really was that much of a saint. She was bad. A car accident couldn't kill her. But when I saw that smiling, closed-eye saint in the box, I knew she was dead.

Snap.

Silence. And dark.

Did I want to go on? The eyes of the doll would open crossed. Doubles, blurs, lack of distinction, everything bleeding into everything else. Maybe I could just stay here, in this place where I'd had a friend, and she'd died, and yes I'd been fucked up and fucked around but I'd pushed back too. I'd been able to find pleasure too. The flower had kept opening.

That was better; this was better, this place, right? I liked this story better.

Tonight's the night.

When the light and music flooded in, I looked down and yeah, the doll's eyes were crossed. But mine weren't. I could see just fine. I could hear that song, "Tonight's the Night." It had just started, down the hall at the fundraiser. I knew Marnie would probably dance, in a friendly fashion, with one of the guys, both of them hamming it up because Marnie was funny that way, could make you laugh.

Marnie made me laugh.

As one said, when a child, *I like you. Want to be friends?*

Meaning, *When I'm around you I want to get to know you, better and better and better. You are more interesting than anybody else on the face of this earth. I think of you all the time, whether you are around or not. You make me scared and happy. I want to show you things and I want to tell you things.*

I walked out of the empty classroom, down the hall to the gym. I found Marnie, sitting on the side with her rainbow-socked feet, and I asked her to dance to that slow, terrible, ridiculous, unsuitable tonight's the night song, and she said yes. I sat in an ordinary chair next to her decorated one with wheels, and we put our arms around each other, and we danced.

MARTINIS, MY DEAR, ARE DANGEROUS

Underwater, everybody is "disabled." Everybody needs adaptive equipment to dive: to breathe, to swim. So, making further adaptations is just one extra step.

That's what I was saying to myself as I wheeled into my first diving instruction session at the pool.

I'd taken to stubbornly refusing to tell people in advance about my disability. Maybe this is an angrily defiant phase all people who suddenly find themselves using a wheelchair go through; I don't know. I just know I started doing it. Restaurants, for example. I'd make a reservation, arrive in my chair, and then make a big deal about not being able to get into the goddamn place (or, as is often the case, to the bathroom). Useful? Probably not. Satisfying? To me, yes, somewhat. In those moments people didn't look at me with pity. But they fucking looked at me, oh yes they did. Some of them hated me. Good.

So I showed up to this lesson all ready for a fight. Instead, I get this sweet young woman with long, red, curly hair, just like my sister, just like my mother, just like. Except I think she really *is* pretty, doesn't just look that way (to invoke that terrible song). And she says, Oh, I'm so sorry, ma'am, I don't have my HSA certification. Would you like to train with Petrov?

There's special scuba-diving training for the disabled?

Reader, there is.

Let's fast-forward a year to my first real outside-the-swimming-pool scuba session. Tobermory, Bruce Peninsula, Lake Huron. Serious shit. Tobermory, Ontario wears a borrowed name. The original town lurks in Scotland, on the Isle of Mull.

The town's name is derived from the Gaelic Tobar Mhoire: "Mary's well." Legend has it that the wreck of a Spanish galleon, laden with gold, lies somewhere in the mud at the bottom of Tobermory Bay: a member of the defeated Spanish Armada fleeing the English fleet. A local witch, Dòideag,_cast a spell, the ship caught fire, and the gunpowder magazine exploded, sinking the vessel. No one has ever managed to find any significant treasure.

—www.tobermoryuk.co

Why did Dòideag do it? Nobody knows. The lesson here: Don't piss off a witch.

Ontario's Tobermory is maggoty (as my Newfoundland grandmother used to say) with wrecks as well. That's why the dive shop is here, that's why the Magical Mermaids are here, that's why we're here.

Reader, we are here for treasure.

There's a group of us, a ragtag bunch who all "graduated" with water wings from dive instruction in Toronto. With us is Petrov, our dive instructor; he organized this trip,

300 kilometres north-west of Toronto, hired an accessible minivan and everything. We arrive, meet the local dive master, Petrov checks our gear, and we waltz onto a hired boat which is going to take us out to a shipwreck, one shallow enough that even we beginners can dive down to it. I am the only gimp in the group.

"Hey, teach?" It isn't a lesson, but I have taken to bugging Petrov because he acts as if every goddamn thing one does in life is a test. "Hey, teach? What do we have to do to pass?"

"Come back," Petrov says.

As we leave shore, I spot a row of girls on a beach. They talk and laugh; they have long hair, they are effortlessly girly. They appear to be making some kind of craft project with beads, and instead of lower limbs they have brightly coloured tails, like fish tails. These look suspiciously to be made of the same material as a wetsuit. I point them out to the boat pilot, and he says, "It's the Magical Mermaid Camp." He says this as if I will, of course, have heard all about the Tobermory Magical Mermaid Camp and he is slightly embarrassed on my behalf at this obvious lapse in memory.

"Magical Mermaid Camp?"

"It's a summer camp. They do stand-up paddle boarding and crafts and shit." He realizes he has said *shit* and turns red.

"How can they do stand-up paddle boarding?"

"Huh?"

"They stand on their tails, or what?"

He laughs uncertainly and squints out across the water like he is very, very concerned about where the boat is going.

Behind us, across the water, even over the noise of the boat engine, I hear the mermaids laughing, each to each.

Diving in a pool is all about the learning curve: equipment, safety procedures, checks.

Diving in a Great Lake is something else.

I am tricked out in my Darkfin gloves (there are webs between the fingers to give me more push-pull), along with the standard Self-Contained Underwater Breathing Apparatus gear every scuba diver needs: mask, regulator, air tanks, fins, buoyancy control systems. It's heavy. I have additional weights on my legs to keep them from floating once I'm in the water. Petrov is my dive buddy and I am his. We will, once in, hold on to opposite ends of a tow line. We will check in at regular intervals. If we are all right we will give the OK sign (not a thumbs-up: that means, "I want to go up"). I've done this in pools, over and over. But…

I haul my carcass out of my chair, weighed down with all my gear and I perch on the edge of the boat and know that the next thing is to make myself fall backwards, head-first, into the water, arms wrapped around my gear like Ripley in that terrible third *Aliens* movie, falling backward into the fire…

It's a beautiful day. I haven't mentioned that. It's sunny and the water is insanely turquoise, and the wreck we are here to see isn't from the *Spanish Armada*, but it's a wreck all the same; a steamer called the *Wetmore* which strikes me as just the name you'd give a ship if you wanted to doom it to sinking, that or it should be the *World Lesbian Flagship*, and the *Wetmore* is so close that it almost feels like I will dash my skull open on its enormous boiler when I fall…

"What is taking you so long?" Every sentence sounds like you could append the word *asshole* when it is said in a Russian accent.

"My entrance," I say.

"Entrance?"

"I'm getting into the water."

"No, you are not. You are shifting around like weird."

"It's hard, okay?"

"Just get in the water. It doesn't matter." *Asshole.*

I glare at Petrov through my mask, twist sideways, and flop into the water like a dead carp.

It's cold.

There are bubbles streaming behind me. No, that's above me. That way is up.

I am suspended inside the turquoise.

I let myself sink through the water, find a point where I can be suspended. Neutral buoyancy. This is better. No hurry, not right now. Just this. Just waiting for Petrov.

There are no sides in a Great Lake. No painted stripes and numbers on the bottom.

It's a Great Lake.

The steamer is right there, just like in the pictures we've studied. I reach out toward the huge boiler, but don't touch it; it might be sharp. A fish swims out and I almost flinch – almost, but not quite. My darkfin gloves make my hands look like those of a super-villain. BatGimp, I dub myself.

I wave my BatGimp™ hand in front of my face and want to laugh. It is so quiet down here, so lovely. I can see the others spread out along the wreck, can see a school of pale, unidentified fish, the bottom of our tour boat. There's a big splash and I know it's Petrov. I wait for him to settle into the water, then swim for the end of the tow line. He gives me the OK sign, a question and, like I'm supposed to, I give the OK sign back.

I feel amazing. Tranquil, suspended. Held.

And then I let go of the tow, and spin, turning around and around in the water, making myself dizzy, like I used to do when I was a little kid. Flashes of colour whirl around me. It is the Magical Mermaids. They have left their beaded crafts, they have dived into the water and swum out to greet me, and now they swim around me and laugh.

One of them leaves her sisters and comes to twine around my legs. I can't feel her of course, but I can see her. She is smiling. She has long, curly, red hair, like my sister. She takes hold of one of my ankles and pulls me down, down onto the lake's floor, and holds me there. I can't shake off her grasp. She holds me, trapped. I will die. I look into her laughing face. I am happy.

That night, back in Toronto, Petrov tells me off about letting go of the tow, I apologize and promise I'll never do it again, and then he and I get destroyed on vodka.

Something he does after Drink Number Three – a sort of wave of his hand as he orders another round – makes me suddenly realize that Petrov is playing for the team. Or the other team. Not my team, but... you know what I mean.

"Petrov, you're gay," I say with my typical tact. I am flabbergasted. My gaydar until this moment has pinged not at all.

"Ya."

His Russian accent has become thicker with each drink, like we are sinking slowly through the strata of his linguistic accomplishments.

"Me, too."

He snorts vodka out of his nose, which makes his eyes stream. This is Petrov laughing. "Ya, no kidding, never would I guess that. You are so feminine, so dainty."

"Shaddap."

"Is why I come here – came here. Russia isn't so good for people like us."

"Here's to people like us."

A vodka or two later:

"What the hell's your first name? You must have a first name, right?"

"Petrov."

"Fuck off."

I laugh and the world slides sideways a bit.

I tell him about the red-haired mermaid, although I don't tell him about my sister.

"Rusalka."

"Rusky what?"

"Rusalka. We have these. Red-haired girls who are murdered, or end their own lives, before their wedding day. They live in water and lure men in and drown them."

Jesus.

"Sounds like the collectively guilty conscience of a violently patriarchal culture to me."

"Sure. Did she say your name?"

"What?"

"Did she say your name? They know your name."

She hadn't said my name, and I am suddenly filled with sadness.

No, not sadness. I am filled with a sense of strangeness on earth. How will I ever feel at home here?

"You will be okay. You have animal helper." He points at his own chest.

"Petrov, what the hell are you talking about?"

"In fairy tales. As long as you have an animal helper, you are OK."

"You are not an animal, Petrov. You are a human being!"

Blank look.

"*The Elephant Man?*"

"I am not an elephant, I am bear!" he yells.

As Don Marquis would say, reader, sometimes I think our friend Petrov is a trifle *too* gay.

When I wake up in the morning and do my daily lower-body check, I find a bruise shaped like a handprint on my ankle. Like the bruise I found long ago on my sister's throat.

Dad can't even speak. We called the police, but they aren't doing anything and anyway, I think the chief's son is one of the ones who did it to her

I tried to take Miranda with me when I left the field party but "Get away from me, freak!" she kept saying, and the jocks stood around and laughed

The doctor said there's no damage and she'll be able to have babies later on when she wants to, like that's the fucking main point of life

Mom's useless, of course, just drinking. Then she went off and she's with HIM, she thinks she's so clever and secret, but you'd have to be a fucking idiot not to know about IT

I want to fucking kill those guys

I'm so fucking mad at her for not coming home with me. Why didn't I make her?

—journal entry, age 15

There's a culture in scuba diving, as in any obsession – for these fuckers are obsessed, make no mistake about it. Addicted. Insane. But of all the kinds of divers and diving, the absolute craziest, the most extreme, the ones the other divers look on with a sort of head-shaking grudging respect, are the cave divers.

They say creepy shit like, "The cave tried to keep us today," and you know, if something goes wrong, they can't swim up. They have to go out the way they came in. That's a long way, sometimes.

You've really got to be insane to be one of those.

So, I've decided I'll become the world's first legless cave diver.

(Of course, I have my legs. They just aren't any use to me at present. So I call myself legless. Reminds me of the old days, the field parties before field parties became a war zone, when we'd drink ourselves – you've got it – legless. It cheers me up.)

(No, I don't Google "disabled cave divers" to find out if some fucker has already beat me to the title. I don't want to know.)

Slept on the flight; Gravol and gin. Hallucinatory dream of M – wearing a silver sequined dress – a man picking her up like a bride and the dress grew long, longer, until it swirled behind her like a silver tail. She was laughing or terrified, I couldn't tell which. They disappeared through a doorway, into the water. The house was underwater. I tried to go after them then remembered I couldn't walk.

My first dream where I can't. 5 years.

She Who Will Not Be Named sent another poison text – wants to be maintained in the lifestyle to which she has very much become fucking accustomed…

—journal entry, present day, written on the tarmac in St. John's, Newfoundland while awaiting deplaning as they call it. As in, for most people and in my own days of yore, walking off the plane and now, for me, consisting of waiting to have my titanium travel chair brought to me, thank you very much.

We won't continue with all the filthy things I then go on writing about my ex. (She just couldn't *handle* it, wiping my ass in hospital just wasn't *sexy*, yes, I think I married a version of my own *mother*, God help me…)

I've left my father at his Toronto condo, under excellent care. I am on my way to Bell Island. I have told my father I am on a business trip – lots of those in my previous life, the life he doesn't know I've left behind, and so it's believable.

I am on my way to Bell Island because Bell Island, Newfoundland, just a short ferry ride from a place that wears its history on its sleeve by being named Portugal Cove, has abandoned mines, lots of them. And they are flooded, and one can dive in them.

Background information:

My mother is less relevant to the present story than the others. She still floats in and out of my father's life, I gather; less, now, since his diagnosis. Caregiving never really was her bag. So, less about her then, and more about the others. My beautiful sister, Miranda, recovered physically from the attack and her teenaged wildness turned into the kind of political extremism that is never satisfied. Anti-poverty activism led to vandalism led to jail time led to more extremism; work for various environmental groups, always ending in a dramatic exit; and last I heard she was setting off bombs beneath oil pipelines. Yes, I take that personally.

My father is very ill: pancreatic cancer. Right now we're spending my future, he and I. He doesn't know that. For the first time since I came out at the age of twenty-one, I have a secret from my father. He doesn't know that right around the time I began my diving lessons I quit my job, and ever since have been living – and paying for his full-time care – from my ill-gotten oil-exec investments.

The paraplegia? Yes, people always want to know "what happened." Five years ago, I was in a car accident. When my sister visited me at the hospital – first time I'd seen her in a very long time – she couldn't resist pointing out that a car had almost killed me. The *irony* of it, she said. Because... yes, you get it immediately. Because I am an *oil executive*.

But I am not. Between jobs? What it feels like is this: I am between lives.

Five years.

I wait to wake up.

Over 16 square kilometres with 100 of kms of mine tunnels plunge beneath Bell Island and under the sea floor of Conception Bay where WWII wrecks reside. Abandoned decades ago, these mine passages are now flooded. Exploration of these passages revealed a trove of artifacts and the cultural history of mining. The tunnels contain mining relics, pipes, heavy equipment and remarkable graffiti that tell the story of miners who died during their work on Bell Island...

—National Geographic Society of Canada

Reader, when I researched cave dives to which I could physically GET, there weren't very many fucking goddamn options. But it transpires that the ferry from Portugal Cove to Bell Island is accessible. The entrance to the mines is through an accessible museum, and while there is a short flight of stairs leading into the mines proper, the nice lady on the phone assured me that some stout fellas would get me down the stairs, *me love*.

"I'm pretty big," I said. Miranda got the petite-and-pretty genes in the family.

The woman laughed. "So am I, me love. We'll get you down."

My mother is from Newfoundland. This may surprise you, although I have already referred to my "Newfoundland grandmother." Many people have a notion of all Newfoundlanders being these fuzzy, happy, friendly people. My mother is a brittle, brilliant, narcissistic asshole. But we did make the occasional foray "home" in the "summers" (a.k.a. the brief two weeks on that awful island when you might actually see the sun). Her parents were originally from Bell Island. Her father was an iron ore miner, before they closed the last of the mines in 1966. Typical in the history of Newfoundland, the mines had never been owned and run by Newfoundlanders so when it got expensive to extract the ore, the outside interests simply closed things down.

Just like the offshore oil fields in more recent history.

My grandparents moved to a place called Paradise. It isn't.

I don't remember much about them except a rather exquisite sense that they embarrassed my mother.

But in all those trips home we never visited Bell Island itself.

Here's to you, Ma and Poppy.

Three words about drinking and diving.
Don't do it.

Nitrogen Narcosis: a reversible alteration in consciousness that occurs while diving at depth.
—*Wikipedia*, the free encyclopedia

If you are drunk – or even hung over – it gets worse. Except – it feels really fucking good. To me, anyway – other people get anxious or have trouble seeing. Me, it makes me feel tranquil, and powerful. Master-of-the-universe powerful. It occurs because of breathing gases under elevated pressure. You won't experience it in shallow dives. But as soon as you go deep, there it is. Every single person who dives experiences it. You do not become immune.

Petrov called it Martini's Law. Narcosis, he said, results in impairment more or less equivalent to the feeling you get after drinking one martini for every ten metres you descend below a 20-metre depth.

Martinis, my dear, are dangerous.
Have two at the very most.
Three and you're under the table.
Four and you're under the host.
—www.slate.com/articles/life/drink/features/2013/ martini_madness_tournament/sweet_16/dorothy_parker _martini_poem_why_the_attribution_is_spurious.html
Too bad. The idea of her writing it is so appealing. And wouldn't you like to sit and drink four martinis with Dorothy Parker?

The mines have been explored to a depth of seventy metres.
That's five martinis. Five martinis is too many martinis.

I am staying at a new hotel across from an old Methodist church just up from the harbour. It could be anywhere in the world. There are large portraits of rock stars on the walls, and the restaurant and bar are fully accessible with fully accessible washrooms, take note disabled travellers. There is an excellent wine list and martini menu. There is an excellent if very young staff. The rooms are everything a hotel room should be. I celebrate my arrival in St. John's. I drink five martinis. Even while wildly drunk I am able to empty my urostomy bag without spilling a drop.

Another legless dream. Driving the car with Dad. The accident. Him passing out suddenly in the passenger seat, just like it happened and I'm yelling DAD, DAD but this time, I remember that I can't use my legs anymore. What the hell am I doing driving? And I'm drunk, too? We drive into a wall, but it's a wall of water. Green as poison.

—journal entry, present day

Thought I was drunk enough to avoid dreams.

I meet up with Petrov at the ferry terminal in Portugal Cove. I am late, because the accessible taxi I booked weeks ago to get me from St. John's to the ferry terminal failed to materialize. I tore the ear off the dispatcher and got myself a ride, but not fast enough to prevent me from being the last one to the ferry.

Petrov is standing on the wharf. He's been here for a week already, now. Told me he's always wanted to check out the mines; a buddy of his was part of the Geographic Society's initial explorations and studies in decompression sickness. I suspect he feels sorry for me. But no. One thing I've learned is, divers all just want the dive. If it takes hauling a dead carp around, so be it.

He is looking for me and looking worried. It's almost heartwarming. I've never seen Petrov look worried before; the man's got a face like a cliff wall.

I am hung over. I should call the dive. There's no shame in calling the dive.

You must abort if something is wrong. That moment when you have almost reached the treasure — but you know you have to abort — and do? That is what separates the ones who come back from the ones who do not. (Asshole.)
—Petrov

I do not call the dive.

Everything takes time, when you use a wheelchair. The door to the taxi opens slowly. The ramp lowers slowly. I don't wheel down the ramp fucking slowly, however. I shoot out like a round from an AK-47, yelling at the taxi driver that his company is paying him not me, by God, and if he doesn't like it…

I hurtle down the steeply sloped road to the wharf and as filled with rage as I am, I almost hope the driver doesn't hear the filthy rest of what I say.

The ferry operators are literally beginning to raise the on-ramp.

"Lower that ramp, you sons of bitches!"

They lower the ramp.

Petrov does not offer to push me onto the ferry and I am glad. Personally — not speaking for all and sundry in a chair, just for myself here, although I'd be surprised if anybody would disagree — I hate it when people manhandle my chair without asking. This happens more than you would expect.

The ferry lurches toward the red, red island rising out of the slate-coloured waters of Conception Bay.

It's humiliating being carried down the stairs, and some brawny local whacks my titanium chair off the side of the huge corrugated metal tube that leads us to the mines, a terrible clatter. It takes three men to haul me down. Petrov takes my feet. I am glad – he knows I can't feel down there, will be careful.

It's a relief to settle back into my chair.

The dive master is trying her best not to be uncomfortable with the reality of me. "We've explored the mines down to a depth of seventy metres," she says. "But there's lots more to explore! The mine itself is eighteen hundred feet deep. It's a maze of tunnels." She's my generation and freely mixes metric and imperial. We've already had an extensive overview of diving in the mines, a safety protocol review, and been read the riot act about straying from the yellow lines that mark explored territory. We aren't to stir up the fine dust that coats the mine face ("face" is what the miners called the floor); it will obscure our vision and fuck with our equipment.

This mine closed in 1949, same year Newfoundland, broken by World War II, gave up nationhood and joined Canada. After that, the mines flooded with fresh water. The ocean presses above us, above this blood-red rock.

It's dark down here. The dive leader turns off her light and encourages us to do the same. Dark. Totally, completely dark. The early miners used candles on their hats, for Christ's sake. Candles, or seal-oil lamps. Boys worked down here. Ponies.

We all have three lights on us – one to use, and two backups.

We all know the rule of thirds – a third of our air to get to our destination, a third to get back. Because the final third is for if anything goes wrong.

The water is very cold, colder than Tobermory. Graveyard cold.

Over a hundred miners died here over the years. Explosions, runaway carts. And one diver, on the very first cave dive expedition back in 2007. Embolism.

It's true. You can feel them.

We swim by an overturned mining cart. See an ancient headlamp on the ground. Vast pumps that used to keep this place dry. We are not to touch anything. Nothing is labelled. I am glad. Petrov turns to me from his end of the towline and gives me the OK sign, and I OK him back. We are moving slowly. The other divers disappear around a corner. The darkness sweeps around us, excepting the small, warm, wavering obloids of our headlamps.

The miners painted numbers on the walls to tell them what level they were on, for they feared getting lost. Me, I fear that I won't.

38. Red columns, red dust. Edges of pillars, broken metal that can tear into our suits. It's cold.

39. I am not feeling it, not yet – that tranquility, that power.

40. A glimpse of the other divers up ahead, swimming down a long, tilting slope.

Petrov checks in with me. He waves – *Isn't this amazing?* – and I nod. It *is* amazing. It is so cold. I'm feeling narked, I know it, but… it feels so good.

And that's when I see it out of the corner of my eye, behind us. A trailing russet mane, like kelp, like hair. A pale oval beneath it.

We are catching up to the others. They turn a corner. Petrov turns after them.

I let go of the tow rope. The thing turns its face toward me.

She is and is not my sister. My sister as she was that morning when I found her drowned under grass, half-naked and cold as a fish in a ditch, my beautiful, nasty sister, muddy and bloodied. Like she'd gone over the top in the wars, and hadn't she? One fucker left his handprint in bruises on her neck. Every one of them left his print on her.

The mermaid with the red hair; did my sister have these long, needle teeth? She has traded her pink, neoprene tail for one silver and poisonous as mercury.

She swims away from me, away from the others. I follow.

I've left the trail of yellow, nylon rope crumbs.

Where is she? I almost panic. But after a few more turns, into darkness – utter darkness – I hear her.

She sings.

You can't sing under water.

I check my air. I am near half into it. I should, according to every rule, turn back.

I am pretty sure I want to come back. But not absolutely positive.

And there's the singing.

Petrov will be beside himself. I am a very bad person for letting go of that tow rope. He deserves a better dive buddy. He always says: *You must be willing to turn around, leave the feelings behind. You can go back to them later. The feelings will wait for you.* (Asshole.)

If you don't chase fear you will spend the rest of your life running from it.

Yeah. That's what I'm afraid of.

I have heard the mermaids singing…

She whispers it then. My name.

What did she do to me?

Mermaids don't *do* anything.

This is the treasure, they say. This is what you long for, long for with an ache that fills your body like water.

They make you *feel.*

And if that doesn't frighten you, reader, then you are not aware, not awake.

Or you don't have feelings like I have feelings.

And that, reader, I find hard to believe.

Unicorn

The Unicorn is a critically endangered mammal of the Artiodactyla order. Horse-like in appearance, with the cloven hooves and beard of a goat, its single horn – growing in a left-handed, helix spiral and protruding from the centre of its forehead – renders it unique among even-toed ungulates, and indeed, in the animal kingdom. It is famed for its ill-temper, surpassing even the choleric Zebra and Lernaean Hydra in this regard.

But it is the Unicorn's predisposition toward forming relations of a sexual nature with hymen-intact human females for which it is truly infamous. Leonardo da Vinci tells us that the Unicorn will, in the presence of such women, forget its "ferocity and wildness… it will go up to a seated damsel and go to sleep in her lap, and thus the hunters take it." Once a Unicorn-woman bond has formed, it is life-long (unless cut short by wanton hunting), and apparently mutually satisfying.

Dr. Randy Fallis, a preeminent animal behaviourist, explains. "A relationship between a Unicorn and a human female involves mutual attraction, personality compatibility, play, and affection. Complex ritualized interactions… show substantial sensitivity toward each other's inclinations and preferences." His colleague Dr. I. M. Horne (herself an outspoken supporter of Unicornist rights, and partner of a Unicorn) asserts, "I am very proud of our work, which might also be the first genuine *Homo sapiens-Animalia non Hominidae* collaboration. We have built on earlier findings, using modern analytical techniques to get at the interplay between Unicorn and human... personalities."

There is wide-spread evidence of Unicornism throughout human history. Chinese women in the 15th century reportedly possessed Unicorns, as did women in late 19th century Zanzibar. The first intact Unicorn skeleton dates from 50,000 years ago in the Upper Paleolithic period, and was found in Hohle Fels Cave near Ulm, Germany. Greek vase art depicts sexual relations between women and Unicorns; one notable specimen, from around the sixth century BCE, depicts a scene in which a woman bends over to perform oral sex on a man, while behind her a Unicorn prepares to thrust its horn into her vagina. Unicorns are also mentioned several times in Aristophanes' 411 BCE comedy, *Lysistrata*: "And so, girls, when fucking time comes... not the faintest whiff of it anywhere, right? From the time those Milesians betrayed us, we can't even call our sweet, sweet Unicorns."

Post-Christian European attitudes toward the Unicorn have, in contrast, been fraught with contradiction. A typical medieval encounter is immortalized in the *Unicorn Tapestries*, more correctly and descriptively known as *The Hunt of the Unicorn*. Woven in the late 1400s, these creations depict a hapless Unicorn lured by a hymen-intact human female; the creature is then attacked and killed by male hunters who have used the virgin as bait for their prey. The final panel indulges in a flight of fancy when it depicts the Unicorn sitting, resurrected and chained, in a pen that would surely be deemed by contemporary animal rights activists as far below acceptable enclosure size. One rare text, more or less contemporary with the *Unicorn Tapestries*, relates a first encounter between a young human female and a Unicorn. Likely penned from a male perspective, it begins with a lustful description of the young woman:

> *A mayden, that fairer was to sene*
> *Than is the lilie upon his stalke grene.*
> *Her yellow heer was broyded in a tresse,*
> *Bihinde hir bak, a yerde long, I gesse.*
> *Hir shoes were laced on hir legges hye;*
> *She was a prymerose, a pigges-nye*
> *For any lord to leggen in his bedde,*
> *Or yet for any good yeman to wedde.*
> *And as an aungel hevenly she song,*
> *To Diane of maydens, goddesse fair and stronge.*
> *O Diane, singe she, pray I you herre my crye!*
> *Chaste goddesse, wel wostow that I*
> *Desire to been a mayden al my lyf,*
> *Ne never wol I be no love ne wyf.*

> *Then came a Unicorne, grete and whyte,*
> *And prively he caught hir by the queynte,*
> *And heeld hir harde by the haunche-bones,*
> *And she cryde, Stede, love me all at-ones!*
> *Winsinge she was, as is a Ioly colt,*

Mast-long his horne, and upright as a bolt.
There was the revel all night til morne;
For thus bedded Lilie her Unicorne,
Til that the belle of laudes gan to ringe,
And freres in the chauncel gonne singe.

Preserved in the library of famed pervert Samuel Pepys (who, as bibliophiles around the world know, devoted a whole section of his private collection to Unicorn texts), the Chaucer-era manuscript goes on to describe the sudden interruption of the sexual revels of the Unicorn and Lilie, as hunters' horns sound in the distance and a company of men, armed with spears, swords, and axes, penetrate the woodland scene. A battle between Unicorn and hunters ensues while Lilie looks on, aghast, with the Unicorn killing several of the party. In the end the beast is defeated, and "from his feet up to his brest was come the cold of deeth, that hadde him overcome." Lilie utters a "shrighte" and falls "doun in a traunce a longe tyme." When she recovers, she enters a convent and takes holy orders.

This work, with the evocation of pagan goddesses, male violence in the midst of female pleasure, and Christian ritualism, reflects a belief that consorting with Unicorns would lead to abandonment of Christian values. Targeted hunting of the rare beast continued through the Middle Ages, and by the 1500s the Unicorn was extirpated in Europe and Asia.

With the arrival of Queen Elizabeth I on the English throne in 1559 came a sea-change. The sovereign dispatched one Martin Frobisher to the New World (the famously miserly Queen even contributed funding to the expedition), ostensibly to find a passage to Cathay, and gold. But Frobisher was "more speciallye directed by commissione for the searching more of this Unicorne thane for the searchinge of this golde Ore or any furthere discoverie of the passage." Thus one surmises the actual purpose of the voyage: to investigate rumours of the existence of a marine-adapted Unicorn in the north of what is now Canada.

Martin Frobisher failed to find gold, instead shipping home several thousand tons of useless ore; nor did he find the Northwest Passage. He did manage to kidnap four unfortunate Inuit individuals who perished shortly after their arrival in England; in another incident, five of his men were taken hostage by an Inuit band and never seen again. However, he did have one outstanding success: he brought Queen Elizabeth a live Unicorn. Luckily for us, Samuel Pepys comes through again, having preserved in his remarkable library a copy of the journal Frobisher kept on the trip.

"At 12 of the cloke," it begins, "we wayed at Deptforde and bare downe bye the Courte, where we shotte off oure ordinance; her Majestie beholdinge the same commendede it, and bade us farewelle with shakinge her hande at us oute of the windowe."

The journal goes on to describe, in excruciating detail and with many a suffixed *e*, the fleet's passage across the Atlantic. At last, after many days and nights of *fearfule winde, ize,* and *fogge*, Frobisher's fleet finally found safe anchorage near what is now known as Resolution Island in Qikiqtaaluk Region, Nunavut:

... an Islande most craggie and barraine, yelding no kinde of woode or fruite, neither any sorte of grasse. We sawe raine deere to the number of viii, with some partridges, bigger than ours, ruf-footed with white winges. We killed one of theim ... On the xxi-iiithe daie, parte of our companie went on shore to washe there lynnen. And one man made with greate haste in a boote back to the Shipp, to report he had seene a faire white deere, yet with a sin-gle horne in the middyl of its hede. My wonder was very great. Could this be the Unicorne her Majestie so directede me to finde? And as I was thus ymmageninge thereof with my self, the beaste came into view on the shore. I commanunded all our companies there not to make any showtes or cries at it, neither yet to show theim selves to it, lest therby it should take cawse of feare and so retire. Capten Courtney and I tooke our weapons, and went a mile to a place where we thought the beaste might be; but it ran verie swiftlie.

The creature was pursued and finally cornered against a cliff. There was a fearsome battle, as the expedition had failed to provide a human female virgin to tempt the Uni-corn; but one Nicholas Conger, a Cornish wrestler, man-aged to overpower the beast before it could escape into the icy water, and it was shut into a silk-lined padded pen.

The Unicorn (or Unicorne, as the orthographic pecu-liarities of the period often styled it) by some miracle sur-vived its passage across the Atlantic, although it kicked its way out of no less than five enclosures en route, and was presented to the Queen. There is no record of their first encounter, but there are many accounts of the Queen and Unicorn's evident attachment until the Queen's death in

1603. During the succession of James I to the throne the Unicorn was, sadly, slain, and its horn remained in the Windsor Cabinet of Curiosities until it was destroyed during the tumultuous and pleasure-denying Cromwell era.

Other celebrated owner/partners of Unicorns past include George Sand, Alice B. Toklas, Marlene Dietrich, and of course Pulitzer-prize-winning American poet Edna St. Vincent Millay, whose beloved poem "Afternoon on a Hill" is believed by many to evoke the post-coital glow which follows a first Unicorn encounter. Millay's Unicorn was a bone of contention between the poet and her sister. "Where did she get the filthy thing? I don't know and I don't care," Nora stated. "It certainly made Edna popular with the ladies, I can tell you that."

How, one may ask, has a creature evolved apparently ideally suited to gratify the sexual desires of sundry human women? It almost flies in the face of reason. With the aid of modern science, however, we are coming ever closer to an answer. Recent studies of the horn of the animal have yielded evidence that not only is the spiral shape of a Unicorn horn well-adapted to dildoetic purposes, the horn itself is actually an innervated sensory organ that transmits information of a pleasure-based nature to the Unicorn.

Unfortunately, in recent times there has been a backlash against Unicorn possession, particularly in Kyrgyzstan (where it is illegal to own a Unicorn or even to disseminate information about the species) and in the southern states of the U.S.A., where much of the anti-Unicorn-research funding emanates. In the words of Moral Ballhurst, "Sometimes you have to protect the pubic *(sic)* against themselves...

There is no moral way to use one of these creatures. They promote loose morals and promiscuity."

Some animal rights activists also object to Unicornism on the grounds that it is bestiality; however, given the evident agency of the Unicorn when choosing and remaining with their human women, it seems more likely that the Unicorn itself is guilty of gynephilia.

Obviously, there are still many unanswered questions about this fascinating and dangerously rare creature. We can only hope that more scientific studies such as the one conducted by Horne/Fallis will be permitted to evolve.

FERRY BACK THE GIFTS

My mother's setting traps for me. Yesterday I found a jingle bell, severed from the cotton-ball head of my Yule angel – one of those mangled juvenile crafts, long consigned to the dump – rolling around in my underwear drawer. A week ago, my Award of Excellence for Minor Divination (Category: Card Reading) showed up at the bottom of my button box. A slip of the knife and a deep cut to my thumb; could be coincidence, but I wonder. And smells, with no warning or obvious source, lingering for hours: freshly-sharpened pencils, wet wool, my ex-boyfriend's body odour (slightly sulphurous); she never liked him. And just once, her perfume – *Magic* – mingled with cigarette smoke and rye. It hung around for days, that one.

The climax was, of course, the car accident. Brakes, just tuned, suddenly failing. Putting my foot on the brake and encountering that… looseness… I was both light and terribly heavy, all at the same time, mind moving fast as a red squirrel, slow as a turgid river. I ended up in a lake. Remembered how she always kept a hammer in her car for just such an incident (she had enemies and she knew it).

Only the powerful have enemies. I don't keep a stinking hammer in my stinking car.

I managed to escape because a window happened to be open. Yes, I know it's winter, but the window was broken, and I couldn't afford to fix it. Couldn't really afford a car either, but that decision was made for me. The old beater's at the bottom of Twenty Mile Pond.

She's been dead for almost ten years. Why is she reaching across now?

In any case, I'm presently and for the foreseeable future carless, thus restricting my employment opportunities still further. I keep body and soul together through various odd jobs: cleaning people's houses; sporadic personal care work; brief employment as a production assistant on the hit TV show "Republic of Foil"; and party-tricks – card-reading, etc. The work trickles in ever more slowly these days, and it's not enough.

Deck the halls with boughs of holly, fa la la la la…

I'm surfing for jobs.

"Wanted: Charmers! Successful social media networking a plus!!!!"

Tis the season to be jolly…

"Curses R Us! Subscribe to our newsletter, or you'll be sorry!"

Don we now our gay apparel…

I don't want a newsletter; I want to be employed. I'm a low-level charmer at best, able to guess at a hidden card, to blow out candle flames by staring at them. As a child I showed some promise as a healer; I can still tell when there's

something wrong with a person, communicate fairly effec-
tively with cats, and find lost objects. My Tarot readings
bring in a little, here and there. But shamanizing as a full-
time activity? No, no; to make a living one needs weather
management, high-level divination or, at the very least, a
good clear cursing ability.

But if I knew how to "brand" myself – as a psychic
entertainer, say – I think I could make enough to get by.
Surfing Virago brings up hundreds of low-level charmers,
shamans, witches and wizards.

My mother hated marketry, those trading in fake
shamanizing and professional bamboozlement. On her
deathbed – literally, she was near the end of the wasting
sickness that carried her off after an awful fight of years –
she pronounced, "If you ever join one of those plastic
witch outfits, I'll come back from the grave and kill you."

People came to my mother through word of mouth,
because she was good. Mind you, her career was well-estab-
lished before the net, before Virago and the other Big
Three. My mother, she was the real deal.

As early on as I can remember, I was an adept gleaner of
wild foods in season, my mother's pantry, and other people's kitchens. My little friends' parents nicknamed me the
Southside Locust, and nobody could beat me for my ability
to pick (and eat) vast quantities of blueberries, chuckley
pears, brambles, and crowberries during Newfoundland's
short, sweet summers. I had knowledge of a rich patch of
bakeapples, and they still grow there, and I will never tell.
It's still hard for me, at parties, not to stand over the hors

d'oeuvres tray making an unseemly pig of myself. As soon as I enter a building, I become immediately aware of all possible food sources: a vending machine, a café, a chip wagon across the street. It never ceases to amaze me when others display obliviousness to food. But then, I am usually hungry.

My first memory consists of making a meal for my younger brother and myself. We were hungry, she was elsewhere. I had been told I was not allowed to drag a chair into the pantry, and we weren't allowed into the fridge (for reasons which still remain opaque to me). So I prepared a meal from what I could reach on the lowest shelf of the pantry: a small handful of golden raisins, two dried apricots, Sheriff's Instant Mashed Potato Flakes, and two pink heart-shaped dog biscuits. They weren't bad, the biscuits. Better than the potato flakes, which dried your tongue to a husk. I put everything on plates to make it look like a real meal. Gave the dog one of the beige bone-shaped biscuits, because she was begging.

Within days I was dragging the chair around despite the prohibition and using milk from the proscribed fridge to make Jell-O Pudding on the forbidden stovetop. As long as I kept the handle of the saucepan turned inward so my little brother couldn't grab it and upend the boiling pudding onto his three-year-old head (an image that transfixed me with horror) I figured we'd be okay. My mother realized what I was up to as boxed Jell-O Pudding levels, which she had bought on sale and then hoarded, dropped precipitously, but she just gave me a tight and brilliant smile. "Good for you, then." And the next time she remembered to go grocery shopping (likely prompted by a dip in her stores of cigarettes and rye, or the need for an ingredient for a spell), she started supplying the house with pre-sliced bologna and Kraft Singles. I don't think she realized about the dog biscuits. We never spoke of it.

She was otherwise preoccupied.

Newfoundland specializes in plain old charmers, probably a last remnant of the gifted of western England and southwest Ireland. Also known as "toad doctors" and "girdle measurers," the charmers specialize in healing, possession, and cursing. Throw in a little weather-manipulation and some legendary flyers, and you have a nice healthy tradition that – while wiped out in Great Britain by the Renaissance, and further decimated by what one could simply call modern corporate capitalism – survives on this colonized island. It's mostly a woman's skill, although there was a male charmer acclaimed for his knot magic; his ability to control winds made incalculable contribution to the great success of pirate Peter Easton back in the early 1600s.

My mother worked on skill-building with my brother and I, as the mood took her, but like most men he learned contempt for it early and turned away, even though I believe he is more gifted in this regard than I.

But indeed, what real use are my skills?

I know few professional charmers. I can spot those with the talent, those other women and the odd fella. They are marked by a love of cats, and seedy crackers; an overly amorous relationship to brooms, and barely suppressed rage at people who refuse to eat the perfectly-edible rinds of aged cheeses. They guess at numbers and often do well at lotteries (a skill, alas, that eludes me). They sense when you are trying to conceal something. They adore sugar-plums and eat vast quantities of them at Yule.

Hours pass and I realize it is 3 a.m., and I have gone down the internet rabbit hole. From charmer employment sites to healer claims for childhood disease cures to a new study on the damage toxic stress does to a child's developing brain to finding six other new studies, and finally sinking to the low of taking, myself, the online Adverse Childhood Experiences Test. ACEs, as they call them, are "stressful or traumatic events, including abuse or neglect." A highish score, they assure me, is an indicator for all kinds of adult diseases and behavioural issues, from arthritis and heart disease to STIs, alcoholism, jail time, and unemployability. ACEs. Ace in the hole. Ace that test. Pass that eye of newt, will ya, ace?

The site reassures me more than once that the study was conducted for the most part on white, middle-class subjects. I am bemused by this insistence until it occurs to me that they are trying to prove that an immense amount of damage has been done to children across the board. For me, say, there was the neglect as touched upon as above, which extended to periods of unwashed clothing and, quite simply, looking funny in school. The alcoholism and contempt. I was molested, by a teacher and next-door neighbour. Nothing out of the ordinary, really; an ordinarily uncomfortable childhood.

Even a score of one puts you in the shade. One knocks years off your life; nineteen, they estimate. What kind of estimation is that? How did they derive it? Nineteen years, snuffed out, just like that. It's laughable. I mean, but laughable. I laugh.

The score's out of ten.

I get a six.

I sit at my kitchen table staring at a candle flame. My laptop lies next to me, closed. The room is dark. The entire apartment is dark, the city is dark.

What is the night?

Almost at odds with morning, which is which.

Time was I could have snuffed it with a thought. I stare, and the flame burns a twin into my retina. It flickers, arcing across my vision. Minutes pass. My concentration wavers. The candle burns.

I sense another in the room, a dark presence, and cold. And that smell: Magic and cigarettes and rye.

There's a sharp *click*, like the mandibles of a beetle snapping together. The candle goes out.

It will have blood, they say. Blood will have blood.

Stones have been known to move, and trees to speak.

Something runs up the curtains behind the table then, a lick, a tongue of light and heat. It takes a moment to understand what I am seeing. By the time I lurch to my feet the whole window is in flames, fabric dropping to the floor, blackout liners fusing and melting in the heat. I have a brief, incoherent thought that the flames must look very pretty reflected on the snowy porch roof outside.

Augurs and understood relations have
By magot pies and choughs and rooks brought forth
The secret'st man of blood.

My apartment is on the house's second storey; I must get down the stairs. I grab my laptop, start to crawl under the table for the cord, realize how fucking stupid that is, and run from the room. Go back for my phone. I reach through the flames for it. *That will hurt later,* I think. Flee the room, calling for Betty. Fuck, where is she? Oh, there, a big black comma on the bed, silhouetted against the white coverlet. Surely my mother won't kill Betty? She loved cats. No time to wonder, no way I'm chancing it – I fling open my closet, grab the cat carrier, and toss Betty inside. She has only time for an indignant *Mrow!* and we're out the door. Whole kitchen in flames, now. Last thing I see as I leave is the silhouette of a woman. It could be me, just my reflection, I tell myself. Tall, wreathed in flames, wearing a dark cloak and standing in front of the window.

The fire brigade comes promptly, and the fire is doused without much trouble. The fire fighters – all men – start to flirt, then something about me (this often happens) occurs to them and they stop. The eldest of them, probably close to my age, has some grey in his hair and kind eyes. He tells me it's safe to go back into the apartment, but it'll probably smell bad. "You could ask your landlord for some paint to fix up the kitchen. He'll have insurance." There's no way Mr. Snelgrove will be offering me free paint. "Thanks," I sniff. Betty growls from her cage.

"Better get that kitty inside," the fire fighter says.

Betty growls again, and hisses. She hates being called 'kitty.'

"And take care of that hand. You want some ointment? Hey Mac, get this lady some antibiotic ointment." Mac gives me a tube from the firefighters' own first aid kit and some gauze and tape. The nice guy tells me to keep it clean and dry, and wrap it up.

I and the other tenants – Josh and his new girlfriend, and Bob in the basement – all troop back inside. There's no damage to their apartments, not even a smell of smoke. The damage is entirely confined to my place, and even there it is merely cosmetic. Nevertheless, they don't look at me or speak. They'll hate me even more, now. There'll be a complaint to Mr. Snelgrove.

Thanks, Mom.

The apartment stinks. I leave the kitchen window open and fall into bed. Betty curls around my head like she used to do as a kitten; we're both upset.

I dream, that night, of my mother. As always, she is big, big as a giantess, or I am small. Yes, it's more that I am small.

We are in the kitchen of my childhood; she is making the sugarplums. She wants me to help, but I can't remember what to do. Always when I dream of her it is like this: me, small as a parrot, and my voice is too quiet for her to hear. No need to go to Dr. Freud for analysis.

I wondered, all the time I was trying to take care of her during the last cancer, if the dreams would change after she died. But they haven't. I am having trouble with the sugarplums. She has asked me to roll the balls in the sugar, but they keep sticking to my hands, unravelling and smearing to nubbins.

"Just roll them in ointment and keep them clean and dry," she says, exasperated. "Didn't you learn a damn thing?"

Cleaning the kitchen takes time, especially since my left and dominant hand is the burnt one. It features blisters and stinging redness. I scrub and scrub, right-handed. Every cobweb is outlined in soot. It's amazing how many there are. I smudge the walls and make more work for myself. I tack some old sheets over the window to replace the curtains. It depresses me. Really, the room needs a fresh coat of paint. I can't afford fresh paint.

Betty is still stirred up, and keeps alternately almost killing me by winding around my ankles when I least expect it, and staring at something on the sideboard shelf and growling.

"What is it?"

Her green eyes fixed on the shelf, she arches and hisses.

I sigh. She sees something, that's for sure. I go over to the shelf and start moving my hand around. "This?" I ask her. *Joy of Cooking.* "This?" Middlemarch – how did that get there? My hand falls on my mother's old recipe box. "This?"

She shoots across the room like a rocket and knocks my hand from the box. The box falls to the floor. Betty exits the room with a yowl.

I stare down at the box. The recipes have spilled across the linoleum, fanned like a vast hand of cards. The box is a tole-painted tin, orange, red, gold, and green flowers on a black ground. I've always adored it. The cards are all the same, formerly white index cards now yellowed on the upper edges from the life-long tide of cigarette smoke. They are all written in her beautiful cursive, an old-fashioned, clear, decisive script. Her domesticity was weird, given her other proclivities, and sporadic. Molasses bread baked in clean clay flowerpots. Molasses cookies, spread out as big as a tea saucer on the baking sheet. Blueberry muffins with the bounty I brought down from the Hill, or even, sometimes, pies, the crusts dusted with coarse sugar that sparkled like fairy dust or snow. She used that same kind of sugar for the sugarplums too. It'd be about this time of year that she'd make the sugarplums, what with Yule coming up and all. I've been trying to ignore the holiday, not having much to celebrate.

"Happy Yule, Betty."

Betty refuses to come back into the kitchen; I can hear her growling in the hall.

I shuffle the cards, wondering if they're in any particular order. I haven't opened the box since Mom's death, I realize, even though ideas about making one of her recipes have floated through my mind; even though I had to fight my brother for the box and ended up just sneaking out with it. Low of me.

But the recipes aren't there. What I see is a heading unfamiliar to me: *Filicide*.

Filicide?

Over 500 children are murdered by their parents annually in the United States, the card reads.

The next card, bearing the heading *Filicide: Canadian* notes that *In Canada, take thirty children each year and kill.*

These cards aren't written in the shaky hand of her last year. This is my mother's writing, my mother in her prime.

One in five filicides are killings of adult children, the next card continues, with a touch of grim humour, or am I imagining that? *making filicide a lifetime risk.*

Of course, the true number of filicides are unknown, for many parent murderers manage to conceal their work.

Seriously, Mom, is this your idea of a joke?

Serotonin is the heading for the next card. *A significant proportion of filicidal parents experience depression and/or psychosis as well as personality disorders, and particularly borderline personality disorders.*

The next card is the recipe for sugarplums.

And the next.

And the next.

Sugarplums, to the back of the box.

Sugarplums are adored by women, despised by men and children, and made only for Yule. She never made just two dozen — always more, giving them away as holiday gifts to all her women friends. Your hands get sticky rolling the balls between your palms; it helps to keep your hands a little wet, and she'd keep a bowl of tepid water at our elbows for just that purpose. She used to put them in little gold foil paper cups so they didn't stick together, and packaged them in wee round flat tins, twelve to each tin, two layers with wax paper between.

The first sugarplum recipe card is marked with cocoa'd fingerprints; a crystal of coarse white sugar sparkles, stuck to the thick, creamy paper. Without thinking, I reach out my finger, dislodge the crystal, and put it on my tongue. The sweetness melts. I can't resist; I crunch down. I realize then that it probably came from her hand, the last year she was well enough to make the recipe.

I end up buying some white paint after all and repaint the window frame and the upper cabinet doors. While I'm at it, I slap a white circle on the outside of my apartment door, about the size of one of Mom's molasses cookies. It works to keep ghosts away when painted on the doors of barns and fishing stages; maybe it will keep her off here, too?

Naw, b'y.

She used to lay on the Newfoundland accent when dealing with mainland clients, or even some of the people from town. There was no harm in it. It pleased people to think they'd hired themselves a genuine Newfoundland witch. Often, the ignorant would express disappointment that she didn't wear a pointed hat, or brandish a dog-eared spell book. "It is not written," she'd snap. And indeed it never was. I have no spell book from my mother, no spells. They have to be taught.

You have to go through the initiations. You have to go over the edge. You have to give in.

I had a roommate years ago, a woman given to disastrous affairs with married men. Oh, she loved a married man, and she was prone to doing things like leaving her thong lying around the lover's marital bedroom. I liked her, despite all this; she had other qualities that recommended her, like a strong stomach for Jameson and a loyal heart for her friends. The affairs all ended after a time – naturally, married men not being prone to leaving their comfortable situations if they can get away with it. One of the endings took her particularly hard. She literally took to her bed, and there she remained. I remember being genuinely worried that she would die. She stopped eating entirely and became so dehydrated that the skin on the back of her hands, on her face, looked like paper. I finally, reluctantly, called in her mother. She, a normal maternal sort, came over at once and started cooking and cleaning, tsk-tsking at our squalor. She got food and drink into my roommate, and slowly, as her body recovered, so did her heart.

I remember feeling mingled awe at her total letting go, and contempt, which I tried to conceal. Awe because I knew I could never let myself fall like that. Contempt because she could. I am like the Ugly Duckling, swimming around and around the wintery pond to keep the ice at bay. A Lady Macbeth who never goes to bed.

Stop moving and go mad, or die.

To bed, to bed, there's knocking at the gate…

What's done cannot be undone.

To bed, to bed, to bed!

Communication with beyond is fraught with difficulty. The messages are liable to misinterpretation, even for one with that gift. My mother could see ghosts and talk with them, although she never – to my knowledge – called anybody from the other side.

Now that she's there – well, what is she doing?

I go online. *Homicidal ghosts, vengeful parent, countering malevolent spells.* The searches only pull up flashy ads for plastic witches – one only finds the real deal through word of mouth. If I could afford it I'd engage a Dukun from Indonesia. Or a Mongolian Udgan, or maybe one of the Obeah women from Jamaica, or (if they would consent to work this far north) a Sangoma from the south of Africa. An adept in any of these traditions could – if willing – tell me what to do.

But another thought strikes me, a cold finger down my back. She's acknowledging – as she never did in life – her illness.

I remember hearing the story – not from her, but from friends' parents, teachers, even a profile in the newspaper that touched upon it. Her plunge off the emotional cliff. The coma in which she lingered for days. The pronouncements in some ancient language, perhaps Celtic, perhaps Anglo-Saxon. Her slow coming back, her change. She crossed over to the underworld. And so she could ferry them back, the gifts. The wounded healer becomes sick to understand sickness.

Not me. I never underwent the so-called initiatory crisis. My resistance to succumbing – my drive to live – prevented my journey to the underworld.

Envy is thought to bring bad luck to the one envied. I think this marked me early: fear of being harmed because people might be envious of my famous parent. I became a class clown as soon as I learned that I could make people laugh and concealed my high marks in school. Even now… I give myself a shake and turn off the computer. There's no way I can afford a spirit-world worker. Those people are high-level, big bucks.

I'm on my own.

I dig through boxes containing old horseshoes, and nail them over every door frame and window, U-oriented to catch the luck. I hammer a board full of nails, and lay it points-up before my front door. I find a skirt with small, round mirrors sewn into the embroidery around the hem, one I procured years ago and never wore. I wear it now, by Hecate. And then, as another wet howler of a winter storm shakes the city, I pour myself a glass of cheap, red wine and set out to make the sugarplums.

Sugarplums are marked by the triangulations of colonization. Cocoa from Jamaica, figs grown in the uplands, cinnamon, and, of course, sugar. Salt cod from Newfoundland went to feed slaves in Jamaica who laboured in the sugarcane fields; the plantations sent us sugar and molasses, from which we made rum. And it was from the Turks and Caicos Islands that the salt came with which to cure the fish: more salt than sugar came to Newfoundland from the Caribbean in those days.

Yule cooking reflects the old relationship: sugar, spice, and blood. The bitter, the salt, and the sweet.

Pus seeps through the gauze on my hand, so I wear a rubber surgical glove for sanitation's sake. I toast the almonds in a small, cast-iron skillet from my mother's kitchen, usually hung from the mantelpiece and dusty with lack of use. I burn the first batch and have to throw them out; I'm not paying attention. I pour a second glass of wine and cut the hard bits from the stems of the figs because as a kid I hated finding them inside my mouth. That takes some time. And I have to be careful, remembering the other accident with the knife. My food processor is so tiny I have to do the work in three batches. In the days before food processors there would have been more chopping, fine as peppercorns. I eat the orange slices after zesting the orange, even though I rather hate oranges. But this one surprises me, juice bursting over my tongue like a last meal.

I top up my glass rather than pouring a whole third cup. It's going to be one of those nights when I surprise myself by drinking the whole bottle, is it? I lift the glass to the air. Here's to you, Mom.

Could there be anything like altruistic filicide? I suppose some parents might believe they are saving the child from a cruel world or relieving the real suffering of the child. Yes, one could imagine that; in fact, there have been cases. But since filicide is also sometimes linked to the parent suffering from a serotonin-related illness such as schizophrenia or depression, one could also postulate such suffering on the part of the child as being imagined by the parent.

Frankly, as small and possibly disappointing as my life is, I want to stay on this side of the ground.

Just because my mother is dead doesn't mean she's not still mad. She holds the poison apple in her hand. She always has.

I roll the sticky mixture into balls, then roll those in a shallow dish of sugar. I imagine what it would be like if the sugar still came from slave plantations. Would it have blood in it? No, of course not, not literally, I'm making things up. I pour more wine. My glass is sticky with fingerprints.

I don't have any foil cups. It's too bad. But they still look pretty on the plate.

I sit down, strip the surgical glove from my hand, lift a sugarplum to my mouth, and bite it in half.

The rich flavours of the cocoa and toasted almonds hum under the fruit like a bass line, the almond extract and orange sing a high note. The sugar melts and crunches.

The inside oozes with blood.

It's a heart, a heart the size of a partridge's, a rabbit's. Half of it bitten out, covered in sugar, it still beats and pumps blood.

I scream, flinging the thing from me. It lands, rolls, and stops. Betty, alerted by my scream, comes running to the kitchen (not, as would an ordinary cat, hiding, dear thing). She sees the thing on the floor, stops short, then cautiously stalks it. She touches her nose to it, looks at me, and miaows.

It's just a sugarplum. My teeth marks are plainly visible, and my mouth is not bloody, and Betty is winding around my ankles asking for dinner. Just a sugarplum, that's all.

I feed the cat and turn back to my wine. As I reach for the glass, I think, right, I should get that sugarplum off the floor, and the thought makes me clumsy and I knock the glass over. It shatters on the floor, red wine spraying out like a blood spill. And my left hand, the burnt hand, bursts into flame.

It doesn't hurt. It burns blue as a rum-soaked Yule pudding.

Now my right hand is afire. *Double, double, toil and trouble.*

The sugarplums have left the plate and sail around the room like wee comets trailing glorious fiery tails. They constellate around my head, setting my hair afire, and also my clothes. *Fire burn and cauldron bubble.*

I hear the small mirrors drop out of my skirt and onto the floor, *plink plink*, one after another. Everything I see, I see through blue, cold flame.

She stands before me, then, in her black cloak. It's not her as she was at the end – she's in her prime, the mother I remember from the dog biscuit days.

"I got six on my test," I tell her.

"Out of what?" she asks.

I can't remember what the top score is supposed to be. "Eleven," I hazard.

"That's rather poor, dear," she says.

"It's not a test you want to do well on."

"You can do better," she says. "You always could."

"Would you just please stop trying to kill me?" I manage.

"Kill you? Who's trying to kill you?"

"You are!" I sound like a teenager.

"Don't be ridiculous."

Her voice! Oh, I've missed it. The contempt, her quick and dismissive rejoinders – I've even missed those. But there's something odd here, and it takes me a minute to fix upon it as the blue fire plays over my body. Then I have it. We're eye to eye. I'm not a pigeon, a wee creature with a squeaky voice. We're talking as two women talk.

"I hope Betty can find her way out of the apartment before the whole place goes up," I sulk.

"Burn your house down?" Her voice drips with contempt. "With ignus fatuus? Are you actually going to let that happen?"

How maddening she is. Rage filling me, I run my hands over my body in a scooping motion and fill my palms with it. I bring my hands to my mouth and drink in the flame like water, eyes never leaving hers.

Ah, now that hurts. My throat is burnt with it, my mouth. But there is less fire on me now.

"What was it? Was it your narcissism, your alcoholism, that made you great?"

"What are you talking about?"

"Your psychosis?"

She laughs. "Oh, dearie, I'm not psychotic. I'm just very good at what I do." She keeps laughing, and it goes on, too long.

I run my hands over myself again, catching it, drinking it. With every agonizing swallow, my mother grows smaller. She keeps laughing, but the pitch gets higher and higher, like a child's, like a cartoon. I drink every drop until my body is clean of the stuff. My last glimpse of tiny her, I think I see her wink at me.

There's no more fire. She is gone.

My clothes are gone too, all except the little mirrors lying in a circle around my feet.

I rub my hand over my head and face, and feel nothing but stubble where my hair and eyebrows used to be. Nothing else in the room has been touched by fire. Betty munches contentedly at her bowl. I am not scarred, and there's no pain on the outside of my body.

My mouth and throat, now, that's a different matter.

I would scream, but I cannot seem to make a sound.

It takes some time. My voice never returns. I am able to speak, but in a grating whisper, and it costs me. And also, I lose my sense of taste. Ironic, isn't it?

But something is unleashed inside me after surviving that night of fool's fire. I won't tell you the exact parameters of my powers, for it isn't done, and besides, I am still discovering them. But my life has become a great deal more comfortable. I am very busy. At times I find it hard to remember that I once couldn't afford new curtains.

Yule Sugarplums
½ cup slivered almonds
4 oz dried figs
2 T unsweetened cocoa
½ tsp ground cinnamon
3 T honey
grated zest from 1 orange
½ tsp almond extract
¾ cup coarse granulated sugar

In a small skillet over medium heat, toast the almonds. Remove from heat, cool.

Combine figs, cocoa, cinnamon, and almonds in a food processor. Pulse until peppercorn-sized balls form.

Add the honey, orange zest, and almond extract. Pulse 3 or 4 times until well-mixed.

Spread the sugar in a shallow dish. Form the sugarplums into 1-inch balls and roll in sugar.

Makes about 2 dozen.

Tightly covered, these keep for about 2 weeks at room temperature.

Warning: If you have not yet realized your gifts, the eating of sugarplums may be hazardous.

No plums are harmed or even involved in the making of this recipe.

THE GHOST OF THE CHERRY BLOSSOM

I sat up drinking with a friend of mine one night: *vinho verde* on ice. It was summer, and long, gold light stretched out even at this late hour, and I could hear the crickets singing through her screen door. The previous owner of the house had been a dedicated gardener: peonies, phlox, irises, poppies, weigela, lilacs and roses, all in shades of pink and lavender and red. Under the not-so-tender hand of my friend the backyard was now mostly tall grass, although the lilacs had thrived. Their blooms were dry pods now. The tall grass rustled in the breeze, and the crickets slid their legs together and sang.

Our talk, previously about redecorating and the recalcitrance of paint chips, drifted to sex and the losing of our virginity.

After dispensing with some theoretical scoffing about the notion of female virginity being a "thing" that one had to "lose" – and some amateur psychological musings about my own sense, one that persisted for approximately two years after my first adult sexual encounters, until I had intercourse with a man with whom I had fallen ruinously in love, that I was actually (albeit only in my mind) still a virgin – she

132

told me the story of how she came to have intercourse with a man for the first time.

And she started her story in a strange way, this very practical friend of mine.

It's a ghost story, she said.

It happened on the west coast. She'd gone out to Vancouver after high school to work as an au pair for some friends of the family and had managed to meet a Japanese sailor. He wasn't all that much older than she was – she'd been skipped forward a grade and so was seventeen at the time – but he was twenty, and at that stage of life the gap seemed substantial. He was very nice, she said, and handsome.

Being seventeen and still a virgin was something she considered a problem, and indeed, she had come west with the definite aim of finding a man with whom to do the deed. Meeting Akio at a bar one evening, liking him at once, and seeing his interest – and discovering his timetable, which left him in Vancouver for a mere week – made him an ideal candidate, for she had determined that the man with whom she would first do the deed must be someone with whom she would never fall in love. After some back-alley make-out sessions, which, she said, went very well, she fixed upon him quite definitely as the man.

Weren't you worried about sexual diseases? I asked.

Yes, she said, but I was going to use a condom. And Akio was the first one to bring that up, when we talked about it. He said he was clean and always used condoms…

You talked about it?

Oh, yes, she nodded. We talked it through very thoroughly.

This was quite different from my own half-drunken, groping sessions which led, eventually, without any real discussion, to The Deed, and the astonishment must have shown on my face.

He was a very nice sailor, she said, and then we both burst out laughing.

Akio was also something of a romantic, it seems, because he took on the event with an almost professional level of seriousness, as if he was a wedding planner or the stage manager of a play. He booked them into a hotel in Victoria and they planned two days away together. My friend got the requisite time off – to visit friends, she told the family; of course she didn't say "I am going to Victoria with a Japanese sailor to lose my virginity" – and they met around noon, had a pancake brunch with real maple syrup (my friend has an encyclopaedic memory for meals), then took the ferry over to Vancouver Island.

Weren't you afraid he was an axe murderer? I asked.

Not at all, she said.

I pointed out that at seventeen neither of us were particularly worldly, although we may have imagined we were, and what she'd done was very dangerous. And what about the ghost? I asked. You said it was a ghost story.

Do you want to hear this story or not? she demanded, and I poured us both more wine.

The ferry over to Victoria was very pretty and they saw orcas, which she hadn't seen before in her life, and she decided they were a good omen because she'd read somewhere that the pods are led by older females. She had a not-very-good relationship with her own mother and was looking for spiritual role models. They got to the city, found a cab, and Akio told the cabbie the address and name of the hotel. My friend then fell back against the seat of the cab laughing until she cried, and Akio became first concerned, then almost offended. She wasn't able to contain herself until they arrived. It was called the Cherry Blossom Motel.

The Cherry Blossom had been a sprawling Arts and Crafts bungalow in happier times, but now sat in a desolate parking lot, not a cherry tree in sight. The roof was graced with a revolving white plastic mermaid, and numerous television antennae. At the door a sign advertised that the Cherry Blossom featured a Trivial Pursuit Lounge, and a Sing-Along Every Thursday Night in the Gay Nineties Dining Room.

"Please promise you won't make me go to the Gay Nineties Sing-Along," my friend begged Akio. Akio pointed out that it was Friday. My friend opened her mouth to explain but, as everybody knows, humour doesn't bear explaining.

I was nervous, she said, and prone to babble.

The woman at the check-in counter wore a plunging, black dress with white lace trim, a microscopic, white apron, and on her head slouched an actual mob-cap. She pushed the room key across the desk to Akio with a wink. Shelves around the desk displayed beer mugs shaped like breasts, and dolls dressed in dirndls, and, of course, a game of Trivial Pursuit. Down the hall, one could smell dinner and hear sounds of merriment; the Lounge seemed to be in full swing, with or without the Sing-Along.

Akio and my friend made their way to their room, following seemingly endless passages, stuffy and carpeted in crimson, up half-staircases and around corners. The wallpaper was red velvet and depicted beribboned Grecian urns. It was a terrible partitioning. They got lost twice and had to retrace their steps.

"This must be it," Akio declared, just as my friend caught a glimpse of something white, fluttering around a corner.

It was chiffon. No, it was a woman, dressed in chiffon. An old woman, dressed entirely in white chiffon, layers and layers of it from head to toe. She was tiny, but with extraordinarily bright, blue eyes, slightly unfocused. These danced over my friend, and over Akio, who was struggling manfully with the key, and returned to my friend.

"Winding sheets are white," she said. Her voice was almost like singing. "I live here, you know. A pretty place."

Humming, she flitted away up an odd flight of steps.

"Here!" Akio swung the door open with a smile and a grand gesture of his arm. It was their room, and the old woman was gone.

About the deed, my friend said a few things. She remembers wishing they could have a beer or five first, remembers being surprised to find that neither of them had clothes on (How could you not notice getting undressed? I asked, and she shrugged), remembers hoping that her years of horseback riding lessons would mean she had no hymen and so it wouldn't hurt, remembers that yes, it did hurt. Her heart beat and beat, and her left ear was unbearably hot. Her mind kept going back to the check-in lady and her knowing eyes, and this made her feel shamed. She also thought of the revolving mermaid on the roof and wondered what mermaids had to do with Cherry Blossoms. It hurt, her left ear was hot, and she wondered if maybe unlubricated condoms had been the best idea. Akio had a notion that if the man did his job, the woman needed no other lubrication, but it wasn't pleasant. Even the pain didn't bring her back to herself. She was muffled in billows and billows of white chiffon. Akio had apparently forgotten her too, blind with his fast breath, straining muscles, gasping with the sudden release of one last tearing thrust.

My friend said she wanted to laugh.

Did you? I asked.

Mercifully, no, she replied.

The next morning she was sore. She watched Akio sleeping for a while and thought about how handsome he was. He opened his eyes and kissed her, but she made him get up so she could clean the blood off the sheet in the sink. She said, "Shall I hang it out the window for the cheering multitudes to see?" but he didn't get it. Then they did it again. It didn't hurt nearly as much this time and she said she thought she could even imagine liking it. Akio was very sweet and went down on her first.

After a shower, they descended to breakfast. Breakfast came with the hotel fee and Akio was determined to get it. The dining room was empty, mercifully, although festooned with cancan girls painted on the walls. She ordered the hungry man breakfast – bacon, sausage and ham, over easy. She didn't remember what Akio ordered. In an adjoining room, a piano ran notes together, a gentle series building to a torrent. The torrent subsided.

Eventually, single, clear tones trickled into silence.

My friend was not surprised when Chiffon Lady wafted into the dining room from the direction of the music. Her face lit up at the sight of the young couple, and she trilled a greeting.

"Was that you?" my friend asked her.

"Oh, yes. Playing German music. Heavy people, the Germans, but oh! They make beautiful music!" She said several sentences in German and then stopped, giggling.

"*Parlez-vous francais?*" my friend asked in her best accent, and the woman went into transports, quoting, perhaps, Proust. She then said something that made Akio sit up straighter than a ramrod.

"You speak Japanese?" he asked, amazed.

"Why not speak Japanese?" the lady sang. She took my friend's hand and pressed it. "I have to go," she whispered, leaning in. "I have," and then she said something, a four-syllable word, in Japanese.

And she flitted away, noiseless over the crimson carpet, between the heavy, dark wood furniture.

"What did she say?" my friend asked Akio.

"She said," and he thought about it. "A, you know." He made a circle of his finger and thumb, and then put his opposite hand's finger in and out of it a few times. "But not rude."

My friend considered. "A rendezvous," she decided. That's what the old woman had meant.

They could hear her singing for quite some time after she left them, winding her way through the muffled crimson passages of the Cherry Blossom.

Did you ever see Akio again?

Of course not.

Who was the old woman?

Well, said my friend, that was the ghosty thing. We asked about her when we checked out. The woman at the desk said there was no such person.

She poured more wine into our glasses.

So I think, she said, that the old woman was a ghost.

Really?

Yes. The permanent ghost of the Cherry Blossom Motel. Perpetually losing her virginity, for all eternity.

We drank for a time in silence.

I noted with alarm that three empty bottles ranged the table. I had work to do the next day and stood up, making regretful noises. It took some time to get out the door – it always does – and I stepped out into the night. The Perseids were falling, I remembered. If I could find a place that was dark enough, I would be able to see them.

ABOUT THE AUTHOR

Kate Story is a genderqueer writer and theatre artist.

Kate is the author of six novels, ranging from adult literary fiction to hard SF and young adult fantasy. Her short fiction has appeared in World Fantasy and Aurora Award-winning collections, been shortlisted for the CBC Literary Award, and appeared in *Imaginarium: Best Canadian Speculative Writing*. "Animate," included in this collection, has been adapted by an international team as a multi-language radio play and augmented reality performance debuting at KUNSTFEST WEIMAR, one of Germany's leading multi-art-form festivals. Kate's hard SF short fiction (not included in this collection) has been featured in award-winning Laksa Media anthology *The Sum Of Us*, and in *Carbide Tipped Pens*, edited by Eric Choi and the late, great Ben Bova.

Kate is also an award-winning theatre artist. Nearly 30 of her works have been presented in Peterborough, Toronto, and St. John's. Kate is artistic director of Precarious Festival, exploring precarity through innovative arts-community partnerships, and director of Alternating Currents, a program dedicated to developing performance works by regional artists.

A Newfoundlander, Kate now lives and works as an uninvited guest in Treaty 20 Territory, Peterborough/Nogojiwanong.

ACKNOWLEDGEMENTS

First of all, thank you to Michael Callaghan. This collection is his idea. I am honoured.

Huge gratitude to Bruce Meyer: veteran poet, broadcaster, and educator, and editor of this collection. "Kate, you should be proud of this. This is a superb collection. There is a thread. There is variety along the thread. There is a purpose, and there is surprise. Bravo." To have someone of Bruce's calibre take this kind of care with my work is a precious thing indeed. Thank you, Bruce.

Thank you too to the entire Exile Editions team!

Deep gratitude to the editors and publishers who believed in this work and wanted to publish these stories in the first place: Brian Kaufman and the subTerrain editorial collective; Bruce Meyer; Hal Niedzviecki; Kelsi Morris and Kaitlin Tremblay; Sandra Kasturi, Jerome Stueart, and Angel Leigh McCoy; Colleen Anderson and Ursula Pflug; Derek Newman-Stille; Heather Wood; Candas Jane Dorsey and Ursula Pflug again; Gavin J. Grant and Kelly Link.

The feedback of Joe Davies, Ryan Kerr, and Janette Platana made many of these tales worth reading at all. And thank you to my many advisors and friends who put up with calls in the night, random texts, conversations that devolved into demands for information, and my outright thievery of our lives. All hail to: the Only Café staff past and present, living and dead; my dear brother Simon the Wilderness Guru; all the girls who survived the perv lurking in the woods near St. Mary's Elementary; Eric Choi; Michael Caines; Ursula Pflug for everything and all; Keith Smith for starting to tell me about scuba diving, and ending up telling me about diving disabled; my father, antiquarian and lover of the preposterous; my mother, glorious diva in search of her best life; Masako Imanaga for essential linguistic assistance and moral support; Ryan Kerr (with ryan knows what and ryan knows why); and last but not least, thank you to my dear friend, Martha Cockshutt: here's to more wine, and many Perseid showers to come.